the Scandal in Honor

By the Same Author

The Lord Trevelin Mysteries:
The Devil in Beauty
A Gift for Lord Trevelin: A Novella

Books set in Miss Delacourt's World:
Miss Delacourt Speaks Her Mind
Miss Delacourt Has Her Day
Lady Crenshaw's Christmas
Lord Haversham Takes Command
The Lord Who Sneered and Other Tales: A Regency
Holiday Anthology
Miss Armistead Makes Her Choice

From the Power of the Matchmaker Series:
O'er the River Liffey

Via Mirror Press:
A Timeless Romance Anthology: Winter Collection: It
Happened Twelfth Night
Timeless Regency Collection: A Midwinter Ball: Much Ado
About Dancing

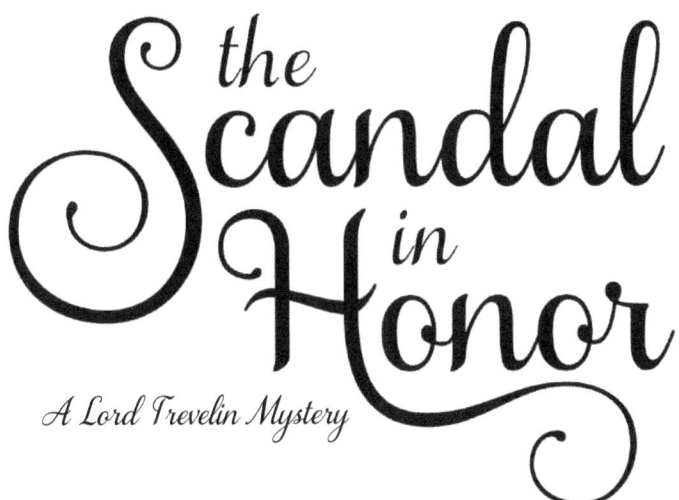

the Scandal in Honor

A Lord Trevelin Mystery

Heidi Ashworth

Interior design by Heather Justesen

Edited by Kim Huther

Formatting by Heather Justesen

Cover Design by An Author's Art

Cover Image Photo Credit: Christopher Bissell

Published by Dunhaven Place Publishing

To Dad, without whose encouragement, Trev would never have shown up.

Please Note:

The events of this book take place two years after those of THE DEVIL IN BEAUTY and six years prior to those of THE LORD WHO SNEERED, currently published as A GIFT FOR LORD TREVELIN.

1814 was a notably cold year in England, so cold that the Thames froze over, and a Frost Fair was held on the ice. My characters do travel to and from London during what was one of the snowiest winters in recorded history. Travel was difficult, but not impossible. The counties involved in this book are of the warmest in the country.

There comes a time when a man must choose to do that which he should not. The memory lies like a flame about to be extinguished, flickering in the past for lack of notice. And yet, when brought to mind, it flares to life, along with the shame...and regret.

Chapter One

The air pierced my lungs like a thousand tiny icicles, but I remained rooted to the spot. Jack tugged at my sleeve, crazy with fear for me, and still I did not move. I thought perhaps I would never see Silvester House, or even England, again. I was in the power of my cousin, Evelyn Rogers-Reimann, and he was not a merciful man.

England February 1814

I strolled into the salon of Silvester House to find Mrs. Smurthwaite seated on the divan under the window, her face pink with delight. Stopping short in astonishment, I suppressed a groan, and managed my best smile, a triumph I am told. (The scar that disgraces my mouth stretches into oblivion when I am at my most affable. As I refuse to smile so giddily into the mirror, I must rely on the opinion of others.)

"Trev," Walter Leavitt hissed as he rescued his glass from colliding into my unyielding form. "How did *she* get in?"

I turned to my friend; he possessed the same glorious red hair and eye for the absurd as his younger sister, Miss Jane Leavitt. That she was at long last my betrothed was one of the few satisfactions I had yet known in my then five-and-twenty years.

"I have only just learned," I murmured for his ear alone, "how Mrs. S. has regularly availed herself of my home." I gave him a hard stare. "It's Hatch! He allows her entrance at any hour of the day or night merely to plague me. I should not be surprised to learn he has made a present to her of the key."

Walter brought his glass to his lips with a roll of his eyes. "You ought to turn him out."

"I can hardly do so!" I said, appalled. "He has been with the family forever."

"Well, she's ghastly," he said, his voice flat. He regarded her over the rim of his glass. "Jane would not like it."

"She is aware of Mrs. S.'s eccentricities," I said with a shrug, "and endures it with good grace." I gave the lady under discussion a slight bow, grateful that she was hard of hearing. "Furthermore, she is not in the least ghastly." ('Twas a bald lie.) "She is a lonely old woman, and my nearest neighbor."

"Shall you not join me, my lord?" she crooned from her place by the window. "It has been long since we have controversed."

Walter leaned to whisper in my ear, never taking his fascinated gaze from Mrs. S. seated across the room. "I believe she meant to say 'conversed.'"

"I am aware," I said, a trifle shortly. No one had endured the woman's corruption of the King's English with more regularity than I.

"She is waiting," Walter said with a nudge to my shoulder.

"Indeed! For you. She has grown as enamored of you as that corset she sports," I murmured as I started across the room to claim my seat next to the infernal creak of it.

"If I must!" he griped, depositing his goblet on the credenza with a perilous tinkling of glass.

We sat, one to either side of her. Silently, I prayed for composure. I had no wish to dissolve into laughter at Walter's antics. He was sure to make a mockery of her words behind her back.

"Now!" she said with a punishing blow to my thigh, one she doubtless meant as an amicable swat. "When are you to wed that sister of his?"

I smiled, my marriage to Jane being my favorite subject on which to 'controverse'. "It shall be a summer wedding. June, I believe, if Jane has her way. She is determined to carry roses for the ceremony." In truth, she much preferred lilies. I dissembled so as to obscure the fact that my future father-in-law refused to allow us to set a date. It had taken a year for him to consent to our betrothal, and another for it to be made public. I, however, remained unconcerned. An older man with an enormous belly, I knew I need merely out-live him, if necessary.

"June? Haven't you waited long enough for connubile bliss? You have been betrothed for nigh on a year!"

"True," I said, "but Miss Leavitt is adamant as to the flowers, and one must wait on such things."

"Which reminds me," Mrs. Smurthwaite said, turning her gaze upon Walter. "You ought to be on the hunt for a wife, as well. That Miss Hannah Andersen would do nicely, I should think."

"Miss Andersen?" Walter said, with an inadequately concealed shudder. "I daresay m'father would have much to say on that score."

"Why? Whatever could be abjectionable in her?" Mrs. Smurthwaite asked with a lofty air.

I met Walter's sardonic gaze over the top of her head. "For one," he said as he thrust out his hand and unfurled a finger, "she's a pauper. Second, she's not had a proper coming-out, and third, it is said that her father made away with himself. I should think that more than enough concerns to render her very *obj*ectionable," he added with a waft of his hand.

"I fear it is not equitable to judge those we do not know," I admonished lightly. Privately, I also found Miss Andersen quite beyond the pale. I stroked the corner of my mouth where dwelt the scar that had nearly undone my life and felt myself a hypocrite. I had reasons for my disapproval of her, however; if my future brother-in-law were to attach

4

himself to one such as Miss Andersen, all that had passed to restore my reputation could be lost.

I thought, then, of Jane; how I had nearly been denied her hand due to the whispers as to the origin of my injury. I concealed a shudder of my own as I recalled that I had once contemplated putting a period to my existence. And then I reminded myself that Miss Andersen's father was only *said* to have killed himself. The actual truth of the matter was unknown.

"Has anyone proved his death was *not* an accident?" 'Twas difficult to speak the words, but I wished to cast doubt on the man's rumored intentions. At the time it seemed the only service I might render him.

"Who's to say?" Mrs. S. said with a shrug of her substantial shoulders. "He fled with his family from the Battle of Blaauwberg in Cloak Town. That was a decade ago."

"Cape Town; eight years ago last month," I said instinctively. As the only son of a marquis, I needed never fear being sent into the maw of war. Instead, I read about it and its attendant battles with the zeal of a butterfly collector.

"Even had he fallen over that cliff through pure chance," Walter said with a curl of his lip, "he was no doubt a coward."

"Perhaps not!" Mrs. S. favored him with one of her swats. "Who is to say he had not planned to return to the fray once he had got his wife and daughter out of harm's way? Miss Andersen was a mere child at the time, and it is said that her mother has always been sickly. He must have felt most protective of them."

"Indeed," I interjected. "He might have been as brave as any other. Why flee the battle, only to throw yourself over a cliff? It seems a frightful way to die."

"And before the very eyes of your young daughter! No, I think it must have been an accident, though I suppose we shall never know for certain." Her tone was wistful. "The poor child! It is said that she attempted to pull him back to safety."

Shocked at the emotion that threatened my hard-won air of *ennui*, I rose to my feet and stalked to the other side of the room. "Walter, shall I refresh your glass?" I took up the one he had left on the credenza and had it half full before he had a chance to respond. In truth, I would not have heard it for the drumming of blood in my ears. "What of you, Mrs. S.? Might I offer you anything?" I splashed some of what Walter was having in a glass and returned to thrust the drinks into their waiting hands. To my chagrin, they wore identical expressions of astonishment.

I turned briskly away again, attempting to collect my thoughts. Instead, I was assaulted by a wave of heat that brought the sweat out on my brow whilst the blood continued to pound in my ears. Berating myself for my weakness, I wondered if I had best retire for the night despite having risen from my bed only a few hours prior. Gradually I became aware that Mrs. S. was speaking.

"I believe," she said gravely, "he is experiecting an epiphalypse of sorts."

I might have laughed aloud had I not realized the truth of her poorly cobbled words. It was not only the loss of life that filled me with sorrow; it was that, with it, the man's honor had been so cruelly eradicated. Eight years later and the scandal-mongers, among whom Mrs. S. was chief, still speculated on the possible manner of his demise. Were there those who yet muttered about the duel that shaped my scar? I had thought not, but it seemed scandal lived long. It was an epiphany, to be sure.

"Don't say that you are distressed on account of Miss Andersen's father!" Walter barked.

I drew a shaking hand across my brow and turned to face him. "In truth, I do believe so."

"The man has been dead for nigh on a decade! How can it possibly matter now?" The foot of his goblet clinked against his waistcoat buttons as he brought it hastily to his lips.

I gritted my teeth. "You yourself are proof that it does. You refuse to have anything to do with the man's daughter, as if she is somehow afflicted." I realized that I cared as much for Miss Andersen's reputation as her father's. It was curious, as I did not know either of them from Adam.

"But it doesn't matter! That is my point," he explained. "What does it have to do with us?"

"Does *she* not matter? Do her feelings not amount to anything? Ought she to be doomed to a life of solitude for fear she or her children will one day commit self-murder?"

Walter blinked at me. "But of course, she ought to be!

At any rate, what happens to her is none of my affair. I do not understand why you should think it yours."

I turned my gaze to Mrs. S., who stared back at me, the expression in her eyes tender. "You have known enough of suffering," she said, her voice soft, "to find it intolerable in others."

"I do not wish to speak of it," I said gruffly. Her words evoked comfort and pain, both of which pricked at my heart. Turning away in advance of possible sniveling, I poured myself a glass of refreshment.

"I believe I know what you ought to do," she said brightly. "Conduct an investiture!"

"And what am I meant to investigate?" I asked.

"Why, the reason he has done away with himself; whether he *has* done away with himself!"

The notion cheered me. An action to be taken was preferable to discussing the matter. I turned to give her my full attention. "Why should I do such a thing?" My show of reluctance was but a ruse; I wished to hear her say it was my duty—nay! —my especial charge to exonerate the man, just as I had my friend, Willy Gilbert.

"If not you, then who?" she asked with a wisdom I had not suspected her to possess.

Walter swallowed the last of his drink with a gulp. "You mustn't do any such thing!" he insisted with a flourish of his glass. "Father has only just got over the fact that you gadded all over town in search of the boy's killer."

"Oh, but he must!" Mrs. S. exclaimed. "Can you not see that he has already determinated it to be so?"

I gazed upon Mrs. S. with utter cordiality. "To South Africa I must go!"

"Africa!" Walter cried. "Is that where the man died? Be sensible, Trev! M'sister hopes to wed you in less time than that shall take!"

"Not at all." I corrected. "'Tis a journey of weeks, not months. I could depart and return soon enough." The thought was strangely exhilarating. Perhaps it was the prospect of leaving behind those who yet wrongly judged me guilty that so appealed.

However, Walter was correct—Jane was having none of it.

"What can you mean?" she asked a few days later as we sat together on the divan in her parents' red salon. "This is hardly the time to leave the country!" She twitched her skirt, folded prettily onto the stretch of brocade seat between us, in a fit of petulance. "There are still so many arrangements to be made for the wedding."

I dragged my gaze from the sweet freckles that sprinkled her perfect nose and considered. "What is there for me to do? I have already agreed that the decisions should be made by you and your mother. I care little for such matters. As long as we are to wed, I am content." I reached across the folds of sprigged muslin (blue, if memory serves) and took her fine-boned hand in mine.

She smiled up at me from beneath her lashes, a ploy

9

that never failed to sway. I began to doubt my certainty. Perhaps Africa was not such a wonderful notion, after all.

"Papa shall never allow us to choose the day of our wedding if you do not show an ardent interest. Why, just a fortnight past, when it had been far too long since you had called on me, he insisted you had changed your mind."

I looked my astonishment. "'Twas before you had come to town to see the Frost Fair. I was not able to call on you because I was bound for London, as we agreed!"

"And what a great deal of trouble it was! To remove ourselves from our comfortable repose in the country to take in a frozen river, only to find the ice had broken when we arrived! The only thing that has rescued my frayed sensibilities is that now there shall be time for you to assist in the selecting of my wedding clothes."

"Me?" I asked, astounded. "Is that not an undertaking more suited to your mother?"

She leaned closer. An enticing waft of rose water and orange blossoms filled my nostrils. "Indeed, I suppose that is so, and yet I would much rather it was you who accompanied me to the drapers. After all, it is you who shall be with me when I don the clothes of a married woman," she all but purred.

She twisted a lock of her glorious red hair around her finger as I gazed down into her remarkable green eyes. In some manner I did not quite understand, I found my lips on hers. Before long, her fingers had deserted her fiery tresses to tangle themselves in the curls at the nape of my neck. I was a man lost.

In hindsight, it took little to persuade me that the absolution of Miss Andersen's father was none of my affair. Not only was it shameful of me, but I was also quite mistaken; events soon proved to me just how very much.

Chapter Two

Several days later we entered the establishment of Wilding and Kent on New Bond Street. Jane wore a thick, fur-trimmed pelisse and from her fingers dangled an enormous muff. I felt certain its purpose was to warm her hands; clearly, I was a gudgeon when it came to feminine fashion. (I entertained no doubts as to my proficiency when it came to the masculine.) And yet, she seemed convinced my opinions on such matters were sound. If I had known the bewildering array of colors, cuts, and choices to be made prior to our having set out, I daresay I should have feigned an illness.

Despite the fact that we were immediately accosted by an attendant who was doubtless chock-full of informed opinion, Jane insisted on querying of me, "What do you think of this lace for my travel ensemble? I think it lovely, but perhaps too fussy for a journey by ship."

I scrutinized the bit of frippery she held up for me to inspect but found I could not be brought to care about lace. "Journey by ship?" I asked, perplexed.

"But of course!" With an intent stare, she dropped the lace in exasperation. "For our honeymoon. Remember? We are to take Rome by storm."

The word 'honeymoon' never failed to draw a smile from my lips. "Are we? Very well, then, I shan't disagree." Her habit of wearing her hair in a series of loops and braids had an air of Roman goddess, to be sure.

Perhaps my smile was too broad, for she blushed. "Please do attend to my dilemma," she reprimanded. "I needs must decide soon, for I want a great deal of embroidery added to many of my outfits. I am simply dying for a military-style riding habit picked out in gold thread. It shall be ever so dashing!"

"Ah! Now there is something about which I can offer an opinion. It must be green; quite green, in fact, to precisely match your eyes."

She gave me a coquettish smile before turning away to inspect the rows and rows of trim lace.

With a sigh, I calculated the odds that I might dine before I withered from starvation, when the shop bell rang. The door opened to admit a pair of females. One was young, vibrant; her hair a dark yellow that glowed even in the watery sunshine. The other was older, visibly tired, and nearly seemed without the will to live. They both appeared to be too impoverished to afford so much as a button at such an establishment. I suspected it would not be long before one of the shop girls demanded they depart.

13

"Hannah," the older woman said. "I do believe these are just the sort you have your heart set upon." She took up a pair of elbow gloves from the table at her side, finest in the shop.

The girl removed one of her day gloves and took the expensive pair between her fingers. "Indeed, they are!" she exclaimed. Then, under her breath, she added: "And too dear. How are we to pay for such luxury?"

The older woman frowned. "Perhaps you shall now believe me when I say that a proper coming-out is beyond our means."

The girl's face fell, and tears started in her brilliant blue eyes. "I do not know what I was thinking. I suppose I believed that somehow we should find something suitable that did not cost the earth."

"Everything London has to offer is beyond our grasp," the other woman hissed. "Come along; I shall show you." She took her by the hand and strode purposefully to the counter. "Are we not to have a shop girl to attend us?" she asked the man who stood guard by the buttons and other easily pocketed items.

He favored her with a glare that slid down his aquiline nose and bounced off the faux mole affixed to the tip. "We do not make our inventory available to your sort," he drawled.

"And what sort might that be?" the woman asked. "The shabby genteel or those whose husband and father is said to have died at his own hand?"

The shopkeeper stiffened. "The sort who demand answers to impertinent questions."

"I see," the woman said, her chin held high. "Then we shall remove ourselves from your establishment posthaste!"

I found that I liked her—a great deal. Quickly, before they had a chance to depart, I doffed my hat and gave the ladies a deep bow. "May I be of any assistance?"

The woman turned pale while her daughter's face flushed. "Thank you, sir!"

"No, thank you," her mother insisted as she tightened her grip on her daughter's hand to draw her away.

"I mean no harm," I urged. "My only wish is to offer some assistance."

Uncertain, the mother froze. The shopkeeper needed no further encouragement, however. He rushed to the table bearing the gloves and held aloft the same pair the two had inspected.

Ignoring the man's audacity, I looked to the young lady. "I believe it is Miss Andersen?" I asked, for she could be no other.

She looked up at me and nodded. The tears that filled her eyes spilled down her pink cheeks.

I handed her my handkerchief. "And this must be your mother, Mrs. Andersen. I am Trevelin," I said meekly. In truth, I felt ashamed. As I gazed upon the tangible consequences of their fate, I regretted how quickly I had abandoned my scheme to restore their collective reputation. The gift of a pair of gloves seemed a small price to pay to assuage my feelings. "I believe you shall require several pair," I said with a tilt of my head in the direction of the table of gloves. "And some ribbon. Blue, I think."

Mrs. Andersen goggled at me like a fish gasping on the bank. Her daughter, however, seemed to have overcome her sorrow. Her face positively beamed.

It occurred to me that perhaps Miss Andersen had leapt to a false conclusion. "A moment," I said, looking around for Jane. "Allow me to introduce you to Miss Leavitt." I held out my hand to her. She lost no time in coming to my side and placing her hand in mine. "She and I are soon to be wed."

Mrs. Andersen visibly relaxed at this news, but I thought her daughter's smile looked strained. I confess that it did my heart some good. To my knowledge, I had not often been viewed as a desirable marriage prospect of late. I looked to Jane who, for once, seemed unable to divine my desires.

"What is it that you wish?" she asked in a stilted voice.

"I believe Miss Andersen is new to town. Perhaps you might advise her on the latest London fashions."

"But, of course." I knew her to be every bit as sincere as she sounded.

With gratitude, I watched her take Miss Andersen by the arm and draw her to the fabrics spooled against the wall. Turning to the mother, I sought to put her at ease. "Pray accept my apologies for the trouble you have experienced. London can be uncongenial. As one who has felt Society's wrath, I find myself filled with a longing to soften for you the inevitable blows."

She held her chin high again, but I thought I heard in her sniff a relenting of her pride. "It is kind of you to treat my daughter to a pair of gloves, but I fear it shall only encourage her. We cannot possibly stand the cost of a coming-out."

"Is there any to sponsor such?" I asked slowly. "She could do very well, indeed, despite a lack of dowry; she is a beauty, to be sure."

She drew a deep breath. "We stay with my cousin. Her husband is but a baron, but I think it shall be enough as far as connections are concerned. However," she sighed, "I fear my finances cannot stretch so far."

I surely ought to have paused to consider my words before I spoke. (I have long since regretted them.) "If this baroness were to agree to sponsor Miss Andersen's coming-out, I should be delighted were you to have the bills sent to me."

She stared at me as if I had grown a second head. "Why ever should you do such a thing?" She looked as if I had demanded the sacrifice of her daughter on some pagan altar as compensation.

"Please, do not misunderstand!" I hastened to assure her. "I have no wish for anything in return. I have a deep respect for soldiers. I was never allowed to become one despite my wish to wear the uniform." The further truth—

that of my own disparaged reputation—was entirely too personal to share.

Her expression softened, and tears started in her eyes. "You are kind, sir, but what shall people make of it? Enough ill has been said of her, already. There is no chance she shall obtain vouchers to Almack's let alone an audience with the Queen if she is thought to be no better than she ought to be."

I knew the truthfulness of her words as well as anyone...and yet. "We shall depend on the constancy of this fine gentleman, here," I said with a wave of my hand for the shopkeeper. "If required, he can attest that we have only just met. Surely he shall promise to speak of our arrangement to no-one." I turned to take in the expression on the shopkeeper's face and noted the necessary amount of greed in his eyes. "Very good then! Allow Miss Andersen and her mother to order what they desire and dun me for all."

The man nodded fervently, his Adam's apple bobbing up and down.

"Under no circumstances are you to breathe a word as to who is providing the funds," I said to him quietly. "I trust you understand me."

"Perfectly, my lord!"

"I do hope so." I lent a slight edge to my voice. I wished to be certain that I would be obeyed. "Not only shall your failure to keep a secret hurt the reputation of an innocent girl but shall possibly sully the honor of my betrothed as well," I said with a nod in the direction of the ladies with their heads together in the corner. I restrained a chuckle when I realized Jane was missing not one word of my conversation with the shopkeeper. Her talent for discretion was admirable.

I turned again to Mrs. Andersen. "It is all settled, then," I said, certain the shopkeeper would keep his word. "I believe Miss Leavitt and I shall leave you now." I held my hand out for Jane, who again came immediately to my side.

Mrs. Andersen curtsied deeply. "I thank you, my lord. I do not know what else I might say."

"Only that we shall meet again." I gave her a brief bow, then drew Jane from the shop and out onto the street.

To my surprise, she was angry. "How can you have done such a thing?"

"Why, Jane, how can you be so mean-spirited?" I felt stung. "For what else could we possibly wish? After all Miss Andersen has endured, does she not deserve the chance to be as happy as we?"

"It must be a great deal difficult to endure a tiny waist and such perfect skin," she huffed, but I could see that her anger was abating. "Or perhaps it is the sad fate of such radiant hair and eyes to which you refer."

I smiled down at her and chucked her under the chin. "You, quite naturally, are intimately familiar with such trials, and many more, besides."

Her arm relaxed on mine in answer, and she leaned her cheek against my shoulder.

My heart soaring, I dragged her, quick as thought, into a

19

convenient passageway. Tossing the infernal muff into a puddle, I drew her into my arms and kissed her until she seemed to melt against me like hot wax.

When we emerged all smiles, the world again collided with my eardrums. The sound of wheels turning against the cobbles of the street was only outdone by the continual clopping of the horses' hooves. From beneath it all rose the hum of voices, human and otherwise, coalescing into a whole. It was a world I frequented, but that had been denied me for a time. To be once again a member in good standing was more than a relief; it felt as needful as water or the very air I breathed. The world was once again my oyster.

Jane tugged on my sleeve and I looked down into her face. "Are you happy?" she asked, though the light in her eyes indicated she perfectly well knew the answer.

"Yes, you imp!" I put a hand over hers where it rested on my arm and gave it a squeeze. "Are you certain you cannot convince your father to allow us to set a date?"

"I suppose I might talk him into an April wedding. In fact, I believe I must insist. The way you looked at Miss Andersen had me more than a little alarmed."

I gazed down at her in surprise. "The way I looked at her? Whatever can you mean? I was merely curious and wishful of being of service to her."

"But why?" Jane asked in a manner I was coming to think of as provoking.

"I suppose because she has suffered a cruel fate, and I am determined to make her way easier."

"But what is she to you? She is a stranger, is she not? How do you know what she has suffered or how to improve upon it?"

"Do you not recall the trip to Africa we discussed?"

She nodded, her expression troubled.

"Do not fear! You are correct; she is nothing to me. It is her father for whom I feel such an affinity." I chose my words carefully. "His respectability is doubted, and for a circumstance that seems as unfair as mine having been so disparaged. He has died, but I feel compelled to help restore his reputation."

"So, she is his daughter—the man believed to be a suicide?"

"Indeed."

She frowned. "Perhaps it would be best after all if you attempted to discover the truth of the rumor rather than raise the hopes of his daughter. However, I do not wish for you to go to Africa. Not now, or ever," she insisted.

"What if you were to come with me?" I offered her my best smile, the one too full to reveal the flaw in my lip. "Africa is easily reached from Italy."

"Perhaps!" she said with a wide smile of her own. She tightened her hold on my arm and we moved along the walkway in perfect amity for a time. When we arrived at a flower stall, I purchased a nosegay of hot-house violets and offered them to her with a flourish. Taking them, she broke the neck of one and tucked into my buttonhole. As we walked, the sun broke out from the clouds for the first time in weeks. It seemed to me then that nothing could possibly go wrong.

Chapter Three

Evelyn Rogers-Reimann, my one-time friend and perpetual cousin, was angry. I had never seen him so furious, even when the Duke of Rutherford let loose on him with his sword.

"You are all the family I have left, Eve. I would never choose to wound you, but I could not allow you to ruin that innocent girl. You know that as well as any. I hope you shall forgive me," I said easily enough, but his behavior meant that his forgiveness was becoming less and less of a necessity. More than that, I had begun to wish I had never taken up with the man.

Eve remained silent as he ground his fist into his hand, over and over, the expression in his eyes angry, almost feverish. Then, quite suddenly, his features eased. "There is something you can do to make it up to me."

I wished only for his anger to be appeased. "I shall do whatever lies in my power."

"What is this?" he asked with a lofty air. "You would go so far as to allow me to do as I like with that girl?"

I stared at him; there were no words to tell him what he already knew.

"I thought not. Very well," he drawled. "Let us agree that you shall promise that, any time in future that I should require a boon, you shall acquiesce. Will that do?"

"Not if it means the despoiling of young maidens."

He waved his gloves at me. "Naturally. Have I not heard enough from you on that score? It shall not be anything so prurient, I swear."

I found that I still could not trust him. "You shall not ask me to do anything that is morally despicable?" I asked grudgingly.

"As I have said..." He flipped his gloves back and forth with an insouciant air.

"Very well, then. I shall allow you to collect in future, as long as the boon you require does not involve anything of which I cannot approve."

Eve nodded and turned away, but not before I saw the tiny smile that played about his mouth.

Adorned in my dressing gown, I studied the two suits of clothing Jack had laid out for my approval. The young boot boy and I had met during my tenancy at Canning House in Berkeley Square. He had cared for me, fed me, and quite literally watched over me when I was laid low and momentarily alone in the world. An unbreakable bond had been forged, though we both would have preferred death than to speak of it. Instead, I asked him in tones of utter indifference to move with me to Silvester House, and he did not say no. Nor did he say yes; he merely came. He was a young man of few words which, I confess, suited him better than I.

"Jack!" I called out in no direction in particular. I never knew quite where he went when he left my presence, but he always responded to the sound of my voice. Within moments, he appeared in the doorway of my chamber.

"Which would you choose?" I asked. I favored the brown, as it was a match for my dusky curls. And yet, being winter, I had grown weary of the color of mud. The other, a blue one, was as bright as the sky was not. I found it agreeable, but it seemed an affront to the weather. Jack appeared pleased to make these decisions for me and I was pleased to see him so.

When he indicated the blue, I let out a sigh of relief. "I think I should have gone mad were I forced to wear the brown on such a dreary day! Now, fetch me my watch and fobs. A jeweled stick-pin would not look amiss."

As Jack rooted around in my jewel box, I inspected my phiz in the mirror. It was a good face, one that had been most handsome before my cousin's duel with the Duke of Rutherford. His was the sword that had sliced into the corner of my mouth. He had felt my interference audacious and had turned his attack on me as frenziedly as he had fought Evelyn. All had assumed me to be the one the duke had challenged to a duel over his wife's honor. The prize Eve gave me for saving his life—a heavy, gold signet ring—seemed paltry compensation for the months of pain and ostracizing from Society I had endured. And then there was the scar...My losses had been excruciating, but I held none of it against the ring itself. "I believe I shall wear the signet, as well," I tossed over my shoulder to Jack. "The one with the engraved double R."

His only response was to turn the jewel box out onto a table to intensify his search. It was an action that would prompt immediate dismissal had it been any other servant. Jack, however, merely earned a grunt of annoyance. Doggedly, he picked up each piece and tossed it back into the box until none remained.

"What is this?" I demanded, eyeing the contents of the velvet-lined box. "How is it not here?"

He said nothing, but I had expected no more.

Briefly, I considered the possibility that Mrs. S. had wandered into my private sanctuary, but immediately discarded the notion. She was intrepid, but not a thief. As to the possibility of Jack's guilt in the matter, I never considered it for a moment.

"Go and tell Hatch to meet me in my study. Stop!" I called out as Jack turned to go. "Tell him to wait for me for as long as it shall take." As I had not yet begun to dress, I expected Hatch would be forced to wait for a long time, indeed. It meant one of the maids would be forced to answer the door. As such, should Mrs. S. come to call, she would be turned away rather than allowed to roam about the premises.

I turned again to the mirror and examined the scar. It had not possessed the power to plague me for quite some time. The lady I loved seemed not to notice it; if she did, she seemed not to care. And yet, I felt it an affront to her beauty. A girl with such attributes ought to be able to count her husband among them.

I idled away the time on such thoughts until Jack returned to help me dress. He had grown enough in the years since we had met to assist me into my jacket without standing on a chair. Since I had had trouble acquiring and retaining a valet in the past (my face did them each too much discredit, or so I assumed), it was a relief to know I need never again trouble myself on that score.

By the time I had endured Jack's too-numerous attempts at a perfect Waterfall cravat, Hatch had been waiting the better part of an hour. The thought of his indignation put me in an agreeable mood and I whistled my way into the study. I was delighted to see that the expression on his face was sour, indeed.

"Hatch, how good of you to wait." I took my seat at the desk. "I fear I was much occupied."

He bowed just as he ought, but I thought I saw a hint of surliness in the line of his shoulders.

"I have a valuable ring that is missing. It is gold, quite heavy, and has a double R engraved upon it. I believe you know to which I refer." I waited for him to nod his agreement. "Excellent. Speak to the housekeeper and organize a search. Perhaps you ought to question the servants, first," I added, thoughtfully.

"I am aware of how to conduct a search, my lord," Hatch intoned.

The notion brought to mind the day I had spent

questioning the servants of the Gilbert household when their son had been falsely accused of doing away with his brother. A shadow seemed to fall across the room, and my delight in tormenting my butler fled. "Of course. Very well; you are dismissed."

He offered another bow and I turned my attention to the view from the French doors that led out to the garden. It was raining. With a sigh I picked up a sheaf of papers and went through them. There were several duns from Wilding and Kent, the drapery establishment I had tasked to equip Miss Andersen. As I studied the notations, it became evident she had not hesitated to avail herself of every sort of frippery to be had.

In addition to the requisite presentation gown and its attendant accessories, not the least of which was the high-feathered hat, she had ordered four white ball gowns, three morning gowns, two walking dresses, two pelisses, a fringed shawl, four pair of gloves, half a dozen bonnets, and nearly a dozen pairs of shoes. There were other notations pertaining to what I assumed to be female unmentionables, of which no gentleman should take note. I did, however, peruse the total amount owed and nearly choked on my surprise.

It was not that I hadn't the funds; it was only that it was far more than I had anticipated. I rarely noticed what I spent on my own clothes, but even I realized such a gift to a stranger would raise more than a few eyebrows. Thrusting the duns from my sight, I shot to my feet and pulled the bell.

When a maid arrived, I instructed her to fetch my hat and greatcoat. She had the presence of mind to bring my riding gloves and whip, as well, and I was off to go for a spin around the park. I could not say why tooling my carriage was a balm to almost all that ailed me, but the fact that it was a cracking piece of equipage might have been partially responsible. It was bright blue with wheels picked out in canary yellow; a real sweet goer. I had ordered it the moment I had been given reason to hope in Jane's direction. I was persuaded her father's grudging approval of our betrothal was at least partially on its account.

The rain ceased, my mood lifted, and soon I found myself driving the road along Hyde Park. It was too late in the day for the ladies who took to the path in the morning and far too early for the Corinthians and other fashionables who flocked the place in the afternoon. As such I was surprised to see a well-dressed young lady seated next to a fine gentleman who tooled a crested barouche. I pulled up alongside, certain it must be someone of my acquaintance. The lady in question turned her head at the sound of my wheels and I came face to face with Miss Hannah Andersen.

She looked almost a different girl from when I had seen her last. Her skin seemed fine as porcelain, with just the right amount of color to her cheeks. Her hair was arranged in the latest style; none of it escaped its pins as it had when first we met. Her hat was as exquisite as one might expect based on the dun I had received for it. The feathers curled from the brim and down along her cheek with such abandon, I was very nearly forced to catch my breath.

"My lord!" she chirped. "Allow me to introduce you to my cousin, Sir Thomas Marlowe." She turned to him and prettily introduced me as the Marquis of Trevelin, a trifle of which I was surprised she had taken note.

"Honored, my lord." Sir Thomas spoke as if each word cost him dear. The carriage jerked ahead with a flick of his reins, and Miss Andersen turned to gaze at me over her shoulder. The tinkling of her musical laughter lingered longer than my view of her.

Stunned more by her beauty than her cousin's boorishness, I realized that she looked every inch the lady. All that had truly changed were her clothes.

I said as much to Jane when next I saw her. We stood together at the Mackleys' ball, waiting for the music to begin.

"That is not entirely true, Julian," she corrected. "She very likely has had lessons in comportment from her cousin, Lady Marlowe. And though the clothing is different, it is the manner in which one is turned out that so makes an impression. At the very least, she has been assisted with her hair and the selection of her ensemble from someone more knowing than her mother."

"We cannot be certain of that. Her mother might very well have been the daughter of a duke, once upon a time."

Jane rolled her eyes. "I believe we should have heard tell of it were that the case."

"Very well," I agreed. The music started, and we began to dance. "However, good taste exists in all classes. Take my

Jack, for example; he never fails to choose exactly as I would, and he is the lowliest of the low."

"Dear Jack," she mused. "I wonder what shall become of him when we are wed."

I felt a stab of alarm. "Whatever can you mean?"

She smiled at me as if I were slightly mad. "Surely you do not intend to keep him on once I am mistress of the household."

"And why should I not?" I attempted to speak in a voice devoid of censure. 'Twas a difficult tone to achieve in light of my mounting anxiety.

"Well, I suppose because it is not seemly. Oh, I can tolerate his presence if he is relegated to his proper duties as a boot boy, but I do not relish the thought of him anywhere near my person."

"He shall not be near your person," I began, but she shook her head and danced away from me.

When the pattern of the steps brought us together again, she added, "If you are to be near my person it is all the same, is it not?"

Frowning, I pondered her words for a moment, then posed my own question. "If it is vermin you fear, should you even now be this close to me?" I gently tugged at her hand and drew her even closer.

She gasped, her mouth open in mock surprise. I could not fail to notice how white her teeth looked next to her delightfully pink tongue. "You mustn't ask a lady such questions," she said with a laugh.

"Then how am I to learn what it is you have against my Jack?" I asked far more pleasantly than my impatience would normally allow. I was not to know her response, however, for the music quickened and speech was made nearly impossible by the ensuing tumult. I pondered her prejudices, however, and contemplated on how they might affect me in the months and years to come.

When the set was over, I returned Jane to her mother and went in search of refreshments. I located the table loaded with drink and cakes and was surprised to see Miss Andersen holding forth in a corner of the room. An impressive number of young bucks clustered 'round her.

"La!" she cried, exactly as if her days had been spent enjoying one round of pleasures after another. "I hadn't thought him quite so disreputable!" Her voice rose, nearly into a squeal, at the end of her sentence. For a frantic moment, I feared I was the blackguard under discussion. Forcing down my apprehension, I joined the group.

"Lord Trevelin!" she cried.

I was surprised by her delight, and more than a little flattered. Then I remembered the price of the gown she wore (a white satin affair with a silver tulle overlay) and my self-regard was humbled.

The crowd of dandies and Corinthians parted at her greeting, every one of them with an expression of sullen resentment on their faces.

I ignored them and sketched a bow for the lady. "Miss Andersen. How good it is to see you enjoying yourself."

"I thank you, my lord," she said with a creditable curtsy. "How kind of you to say so."

I marveled at the prettiness of her manners. This was not something one learned in a matter of days. My opinion of her mother went up a notch.

"You look enchanting." It was no lie. The expensive gloves she had chosen at the drapers' the day we met highlighted the delicacy of her wrists, whilst the ribbon threaded through her golden curls deepened the blue of her eyes. She was a vision.

The sudden color across her cheeks suggested she knew my thoughts, but it in no way diminished her beauty. It was just enough that she appeared demure whilst the fluttering of her lashes demonstrated no lack of confidence. The combination was alluring. No wonder the young men took no notice of her dowry-less state. Turning to them she said, "I find that I am thirsty!"

The pack of them stepped toward the table *ensemble*, and she returned her gaze to bat her lashes at me.

I nearly laughed aloud at her impudence but had no wish to injure her. "I believe I ought to restore you to your mother," I suggested, holding out my arm.

She took it without a single glance for her beaus, their hands full of lemonade and orgeat, frustration writ clearly across their faces. "How fortuitous that you found me when you did," she said. "I have been saving the next set for you."

"Have you?" I could not hide my surprise. I wondered if perhaps she hoped to fill Jane's place in my affections.

"Yes." She smiled up at me, her expression exactly as it ought to be. "I wished to thank you for all you have done. As you see, I do go about a little, despite the fact I have not yet curtsied to the queen."

It was a concerning thought. There was no chance of an audience with the queen before the spring. Miss Andersen was in danger of coming across as too fast if she continued to attract so much attention.

"Whether or not you are invited to private balls such as this is at the discretion of your hostess," I instructed. "However, I doubt you shall obtain vouchers to Almack's until you make your bows to her Majesty."

"I am persuaded you are correct. Shall we dance, then?" she asked with an arch look.

I could not say her nay and we took our places on the dance floor.

"In regard to my lacks, you are so generous as to be seen with me in the ballroom. It shall lend me a great deal of consequence."

Her words nearly took the air from my lungs. How I longed to believe them the truth. Instead, I feared my presence by her side might very well sink her in Society's esteem. I was overcome with chagrin at the thought, and my skin itched as if covered in muck.

We danced, but all the while I felt despair. Despite Jane's affection for me, there were times when nothing could dispel my doubt as to my worthiness. I reminded myself regularly that Evelyn's crime was not my own, yet I could not quell the fear that there were those who believed otherwise. If only they were not confronted by my scar with every meeting, reminding them always of that fateful day! I longed for a means to call to mind what it was others saw, if only to prepare me for the treatment that might be in store.

As I brooded, I thought I caught a glimpse of a friend as he walked past. I had met him at school as a boy. In more recent years, I had known him best as a shade of the man he had been. He was dead, now. I knew that well enough, but it had not prevented him from visiting me. I had not, however, seen him since Jane had agreed to be my wife. Eagerly, I scanned the room, but if he had been in attendance, Willy had gone.

Chapter Four

Miss Andersen and I danced a quadrille, and then another before I recalled that I was meant to bring something to quench Jane's thirst. I glanced in her direction; she appeared to be as grieved as I feared. I could hardly abandon Miss Andersen on the dance floor; 'twould be to no one's credit. To my relief, her mother was moving in the direction of Jane and Mrs. Leavitt. Introductions could be made all around, reassuring both my betrothed and her mother, who looked as cross as her daughter.

"You needn't be concerned," Miss Andersen said, taking my arm as the music stilled. "I have not set my cap for you."

I would have liked to smile my relief, but I was too much occupied with smiling my apologies at the Leavitts instead. To my shame, I utterly ignored Miss Andersen during our entire journey to where Jane and her mother had been joined by Mrs. Andersen. I prayed Jane would be kind.

Plucking Miss Andersen's hand from my arm, I gave it a squeeze of reparation as I backed away from her. I then took

Jane's hand and placed it where Miss Andersen's had been. Everyone smiled, Jane rather stiltedly. I adjusted my cravat to ease the anxious constriction of my throat and was relieved to see another lady approach; Jane was certain to behave herself in the presence of a stranger.

"Miss Leavitt," Miss Andersen said with a perfectly unobjectionable air. "Your Lord Trevelin is so very charming. How good of him to take pity on a nobody like myself."

I scrutinized her words for lack of sincerity and found none. However, it was Jane's opinion that mattered most, and that of her mother. Though somewhat startled, they seemed to take Miss Andersen's words as sincere as well.

"He is happy, I am certain, to make your stay in London as pleasant as possible." Jane then turned to Mrs. Andersen. "Allow me to introduce you to my mother."

Introductions were made all around, including the new addition who turned out to be Lady Marlowe, the cousin of whom Mrs. Andersen had told me the day we had met. She, however, was no stranger to Mrs. Leavitt and her daughter. We were told Sir Thomas had business that night and could not attend. The six of us stood in an awkward cluster for a few moments before I recalled my original chore.

Once again I made my way into the refreshment room and noticed the same young men were still pestering young ladies. This time it was a girl I recognized as having had enjoyed her coming-out a number of years prior.

"She is not what she appears," the young lady (I believe

her name was Miss Hadfield) said in a stage whisper. "She hasn't a feather to fly with. How she was invited to Lady Mackley's ball, I cannot imagine. She is usually quite particular!"

The young men, on the whole, looked doubtful. One, however, seemed utterly swayed by the young lady's words. "I shall have little to do with her in future," he said in scathing tones. "Her father has died, leaving the family with nothing."

"You can hardly lay the blame in Miss Andersen's dish!" one of the others piped up.

"Perhaps not." Miss Hadfield favored them with an arch look from behind her fan. "However, it is said he would yet live to protect his family had he not chosen to put a period to his existence."

The young men all looked suitably shocked but not, I was sorry to note, by Miss Hadfield's use of common slang. Sadly, the others of my party had decided to come in search of me and appeared just as Miss Hadfield had said her worst.

Miss Andersen, eyes wide, picked up her skirts and fled the room. Her mother heaved a dismissive sigh as if this behavior was every day fare, but her face was very white.

Lady Marlowe patted her cousin's arm. "I shall go to her." This left me alone with the Leavitts and Mrs. Andersen. The silence was strained, and I thought about what I might say to put everyone at their ease.

Mrs. Leavitt was better at such niceties than I, however.

"Your daughter is lovely," she said in kind tones to Mrs. Andersen.

I suppressed an overwhelming desire to embrace my future mother-in-law. "Indeed, she was very much in demand when I encountered her earlier," I offered. "I think she shall do well for herself."

"I pray you are correct," her mother murmured. I was shocked to see her face had become considerably paler. Even her faintly-smiling lips were impossibly white.

"Allow me to fetch you something to drink." I hastened to the knot of people around the table. When I turned about, glass of lemonade in hand, Mrs. Leavitt had an arm around Mrs. Andersen who, it would seem, was recovering from a slight faint.

"Julian, perhaps we should send for a doctor," Jane said when I had returned to her side. She took the glass and held it to Mrs. Andersen's lips. "I am hopeful there is one in attendance tonight."

With a sputter, Mrs. Andersen steadied herself. "Please, no," she said, holding out a hand in supplication. "I am quite well. And see there." She looked towards the entrance of the room, "Hannah has returned."

I turned to see Miss Andersen enter with Lady Marlowe and a man I did not recognize. I noted how her mother rallied at the sight. She and the man exchanged a look that clearly proclaimed an intimacy between them. Miss Andersen, however, saw only that her mother still lingered in Mrs. Leavitt's arms and, with a gasp, rushed to her side.

"Mama, we must take you home!"

"Nonsense," her mother murmured. "I have never felt better."

The man went to Mrs. Andersen's side. I could not help but notice how her daughter's face darkened in response. Mrs. Andersen seemed not to notice, however, and introduced him as Dr. Nuttall.

"He is rather like a guru," Miss Andersen said in tones that usually accompany a roll of the eyes.

I disliked him instantly. Turning to him I asked, "Are you, then, a doctor or a guru?" I smiled to take the sting from my words.

His smile in return was perfectly at ease. "I studied at Oxford; Magdalene College. I am very much interested in the healing properties of herbs and other plants."

Despite my misgivings, I was fascinated. "And how long have you been acquainted with the Andersens?" I was shocked at the surge of protective feelings that assailed me. (It would seem a sense of ownership comes, part and parcel, with the purchase of a young woman's wardrobe.)

Dr. Nuttall cocked a brow. "Since we met on the stage en route for London. It was late September was it not, Mrs. Andersen?"

She smiled wanly at him, but there was a fondness in her eyes that seemed too strong an emotion for a couple who had met only months previous. Dr. Nuttall appeared to be pleased, while Miss Andersen scowled. Idly, I wondered if she preferred the physician had formed a stronger bond with her than with her mother.

He was a handsome man, one I assumed was wealthy enough, but I thought him far too old for her. And then I recalled my father had been two dozen years the senior of my mother. She had been devoted to him until the day he died. She followed him to the grave less than a week later, having succumbed to the same malady as he.

It was only a fortnight after the ball that Jane and I were once again shopping for wedding clothes. I could not refrain from teasing her about it. "You need but one gown in which to marry." I looked down to peer into her face, but it was obscured by the froth of lace that fringed her bonnet.

"You are quite correct," came her voice from somewhere behind the fall of mousseline. "I am still in search of a costume to don as we depart the wedding breakfast for the docks."

I quelled a spurt of guilt; I had not yet purchased tickets to the continent. It seemed premature to do so, as her father had still not allowed us to set a date, or have the banns called. "Should you not merely wear the same gown from the church to the breakfast, and for the remainder of the day?"

She shook her head and the lace swayed, heavily. "And look a commoner? The wife of a marquis is expected to make a grand display."

I could not agree. The Leavitts were well-received in Society, but they were not of the nobility. It dawned on me that this could pose a problem in our marriage. I found her father's show of wealth to be beyond vulgar and had no wish for her to ape his habits in that regard.

"Oh, dear!" she said, craning her neck to better see something down the street.

I followed her gaze and, once again, I thought I saw him. My friend, Willy. Upon closer observation, it was not he. Not for a moment did I wonder how 'twas possible to see a dead man walk along Bond Street. "What is it?" I asked, feeling a trifle cross.

"I do believe that is Sally Jersey approaching. Now, you must not say anything in her presence you do not wish everyone else to know."

"What makes you believe I would?" I asked, though I doubted I should receive an answer to this question. It seemed Jane did not trust me to be discreet, for she pulled me into a shop before we encountered the lady in question. As it was an establishment that sold leather goods and reeked of the animal urine used to treat the hides, I assumed we were in hiding.

The shopkeeper lost no time in pointing out the abundant qualities of a pair of boots when the bell over the door rang. I turned to see the dreaded Lady Jersey enter, trailed by a pair of footmen, laden down with packages. All of the talk I had heard about her came forcibly to mind and I was suddenly apprehensive. She had thoroughly ignored me since the duel, a scandal to which she had most certainly laid her tongue. Like Jane, I had no wish to provide further fodder. The power she possessed to undo my restored reputation could be the undoing of me.

"Good afternoon," Jane said, with such delight that I could not help but wonder how many complaints of me her perfect manners had kept hidden from my knowledge. "Lord Trevelin, it is Lady Jersey."

"Good afternoon, Lady Jersey," I said, striding forth to take her hand and bow over it. What followed was a tedious conversation of such length that I wondered why I had ever felt delight in the woman's presence. The ladies gave me no notice, and I allowed my thoughts to wander. And yet, a remark she made just before she quit the shop had the power to draw my attention like no other.

"In truth, I have some news for Trevelin," she announced, shifting to face me.

I recovered from my surprise and, I regret to admit, satisfaction at her interest in me soon enough to make sense of her words to come. And yet, they made none at all.

"Mrs. Andersen has perished, and it seems her daughter has not ceased asking for you, my lord."

There followed a moment of stunned silence. My gaze flew to Jane's; if her eyes had been daggers I would now be dead and buried. Silently, I rehearsed my reply to ensure I revealed nothing that might do me or my future bride any discredit. "I am very sorry to hear this, but I cannot think why Miss Andersen should ask for me. We have only met twice. I believe she must now enjoy the protection of her mother's cousin and her husband."

Lady Jersey's smile thinned into a terse line. "I do not believe she enjoys anything at the moment, my lord. Her mother has died, and Miss Andersen is quite distraught. It is said by everyone that she asks for you." She batted her lashes at me as if in quest of the reason why.

Bewildered as much as ever, I ignored her curiosity and thanked her. I bowed far more deeply than was her due and lifted my gaze to see her already halfway out the door, her perfectly matched footmen staggering after her.

Jane and I watched from the window until Lady Jersey disappeared down the walkway. We left the shop without a backwards glance and were heading for my carriage before I noticed how stiff Jane's arm felt upon mine. "What is it?" I quietly asked. "You cannot be angry with me for speaking with Lady Jersey. The fault is not to be laid in my dish."

"Yes, that is true," Jane said, her tone frosty. "I cannot help but be vexed, however. Now she shall tell all and sundry that you know Miss Andersen."

"If Lady Jersey knows her well enough to speak so intimately of her, why should I not admit to our acquaintance?" Even as I said the words, I knew the answer. I was a gentleman and Miss Andersen a young orphan.

"I wonder that Lady Jersey speaks of such a No One at all," Jane said, "except that the story involves you. She is a gossip-monger of the worst sort. Do not say I have not warned you!"

"I see the danger, (I did indeed) but I do not see how I could have done any different than I have."

44

Jane stopped in the middle of the walkway and turned to face me. "You should never have spoken to Miss Andersen from the start. You have now admitted to meeting her not once, but twice! If any have the truth as to the goods you have paid for on her behalf, there shall be much more talk than this!"

I felt my face fall like apples from a cart that had encountered the pavement. Taking her arm, I drew her along the street in the opposite direction in which Lady Jersey had disappeared. "What of your father? Will he insist we put off the wedding?"

Her expression softened, and her eyes filled with a tenderness that caused my stomach to flutter. "I shall speak to Papa, of course, if it should come to that. As I was present when you first met Miss Andersen, he should take my account of what happened to be the truth."

I was not as hopeful. "People are so willing to believe the worst of others. Am I not proof of that? Something must be done, and as soon as possible." I had no idea of what, however.

"We shall go to her, you and I, together. There shall be no misapprehension, then. No one shall believe you would tolerate having your betrothed and your bit of muslin beneath the same roof."

"She is not my bit of muslin," I hissed, taking note of the bald interest evident in the faces of passersby. "It is too late, anyway. Everyone seems already to know."

"How could they? Lady Jersey went in the opposite

direction. How she learned of that woman's death so quickly I cannot say, but it is not as if it has been posted in the periodicals," Jane soothed.

"I pray you are correct. Let us do as you say and pay Miss Andersen a call of condolences. Whatever it is she wants she can petition me at the time, in the presence of her guardians. Surely, she can have nothing to say to me that might engender scandal." I wished with all my heart to believe it was true, but I knew better the way of the world. It seemed, however, the best means to prevent the worst from happening.

I signaled my coachman to pull alongside where we tarried on the walkway. I did not wait for him to fold down the steps, opting to do so myself in the interest of time. I pulled them back after we were inside and knocked on the ceiling. He assumed I meant to repair directly to Jane's home, and I was happy to allow him to go in that direction whilst she and I concocted a plan.

"Lady Jersey mentioned Sir Thomas resides on Half Moon Street," I supplied.

"He is nothing but a mushroom," Jane said tartly. "Papa has said so. He has no business residing in Mayfair."

"If he has the money, not to mention the title, to do so, why should it concern your father?" I asked in a manner not conducive to reply. "We shall arrive in the middle of morning calls." As they were made in the course of an afternoon, it could pose a problem. "There may very well be a great many others offering their condolences," I mused.

"Who might those be?" Jane asked with a wry smile. "They haven't been in town long enough to make friends— any save you," she added. "Her cousins have doubtless refrained from introducing her to many of their friends."

"But was that not the purpose, for Lady Marlowe to introduce her into Society?" I rapped my cane against the ceiling and braced myself against the inevitable shift and sway of the carriage as it drew to a halt. I began to put my head out the window to direct the coachman to our new destination, but Jane put her hand on my sleeve.

Aghast, I realized I had nearly announced to the world I was on my way to the side of one Miss Andersen, who had asked for me most particularly. I heard the panic in the staccato of my breath and strove to control it as the coachman jumped down from the box and opened the door. "Where to, my lord?"

I looked to Jane and she looked back at me. "Half Moon Street," I said softly.

"What was that, my lord? I did not quite catch it," the coachman said as he cupped his ear.

I leaned forward and put my lips to the edge of his grimy fingers. "Half Moon Street, to the home of Sir Thomas Marlowe."

To my relief, the coachman merely nodded, and we were soon again on our way. The beat of my heart slowed to a nearly normal pace. I relaxed enough to smile at my betrothed where she sat on the bench across from me. She looked breathtakingly beautiful, her red hair a flame against the white froth of her bonnet. From my vantage point it seemed trimmed to perfection, as it made the most of her almond-shaped eyes. I clasped her gloved fingers in mine for a moment and she returned my affection with a brilliant smile. I resolved that, whatever happened, I would not lose her.

Chapter Five

Sir Thomas' home was unexpectedly impressive. We were ushered into a vast reception room on the ground floor. It was adorned on each end with an Adams fireplace. In between was a desert of black and white marble tile that rang with the cacophony of our heels as they struck the floor.

Lady Marlowe, her eyes wide as she watched our approach, sat at the far end on a divan placed to one side of the fire. A man stood behind her, his hand on her shoulder, his gaze lingering in the flames. I had seen him before, tooling the carriage that drove Miss Andersen through the park. In a chair facing us sat the young lady herself, her expression wan but her chin held high. Behind her stood Dr. Nuttall. He kept his hands at his sides, but there was a possessive air about him I could not like.

Delivered of his charge, the butler who led us into this cold atmosphere bowed and went away. I could not help but notice that his departure was silent; a skill I longed to learn, preferably before I took another step. I considered gliding my foot forward before bowing over it, then remembered I out-ranked all of them put together and offered only a generous dip of my head.

Sir Thomas bowed deeply but refused to meet my gaze. Lady Marlowe remained seated, but Miss Andersen began to rise. I gestured that she should not trouble herself. The physician bowed as well, his gaze wary and plainly curious.

"My lord," Miss Andersen said softly. "Allow me to introduce the husband of my cousin, Sir Thomas. I believe you remember him from our encounter at Hyde Park."

"Yes, of course." I turned to Jane. "This is Miss Jane Leavitt, my betrothed."

She dipped a curtsy.

"Dr. Nuttall." I turned my attention to him. "Was it you who attended to Miss Andersen's mother?"

"She would have no other." Miss Andersen looked down into the knot of her clasped fingers. "He has seen her through many a low period. He did all he could for her."

I thought Sir Thomas looked offended by my audacity, while Lady Marlowe merely looked away with an expression I could only define as resignation.

"Miss Leavitt and I wish to offer our sympathy. We came the moment we learned of it. We have only met your mother a few times, but I believe you shall miss her very much."

Miss Andersen choked a little and turned to the doctor, who put a hand on her shoulder.

To my surprise, Jane and I were not invited to sit. I had

been in the presence of those who grieved before (most recently the Gilberts, a couple who had lost both of their sons through the folly of others), but I felt that I had not seen it deprive people of their manners. Then I recalled the Gilberts' unexpected contempt of me and altered my opinion.

"We can see you are still in the depths of your grief. I should very much like to be of any assistance I may render." I turned to Miss Andersen. "I fear there shall be no coming-out for you this season."

It seemed an odd thing to say to those who did not know of my investment in Miss Andersen's role as debutante, but I did not realize it until I saw Jane's eyes widen in reproach. "I beg your pardon; it is none of my affair." I winced. "That is to say, Lady Marlowe is here to advise you in the absence of your dear mother."

"And I am grateful," Miss Andersen said somberly. "My lord, might I speak to you in private?" She rose, her gaze expectant. "Just for a moment."

I looked to Jane, but saw that she hadn't any better idea of how to respond than I. The physician looked alarmed, whilst Sir Thomas and his wife behaved as if they hadn't heard Miss Andersen's request.

Without waiting for a reply, she took me by the arm and drew me a few paces away. As the room echoed with our very breath, I could not determine how this distance was in the least useful. Miss Andersen did not seem to realize it, however.

51

"You might think it an extraordinary claim, but I do believe my mother was murdered."

Her words had the strangest effect upon my senses. I was immediately taken back to the Gilberts' front hall as I stared down at the body of their youngest son. Senyor Rey, a man I had not thought of in at least a year, and his wife, the former Miss Woodmansey, came forcibly to mind, as well. And then there was Lady Vawdrey and her man, Throckmorton, who had died in my arms in the course of my pursuit of a killer. There was more, but I stopped the images from coming before I relived the worst of it.

"I am surprised to hear you say so," I said with a mental shake of my head. "Murder is a most serious accusation."

"Indeed. Nevertheless, it is true."

I stood a bit closer and lowered my voice further than I had thought possible. "Do you suspect anyone in particular?"

She uttered a low "yes", and I felt a chill run down my spine.

I had wished to help this daughter of a soldier who died in such a mysterious manner, but I had no desire to attempt to solve another murder. "Then I suggest you get away from that person as quickly as possible."

"It is not so simple," she murmured. "I am not free to do as I wish."

"Someone in your household, then..."

"Yes. I fear I shall be next."

I felt the blood drain from my face. I had failed to save

Willy despite finding the true killer. Could I redeem myself through the saving of this young girl's life? And what of Jane? I looked to her and wondered if she could endure the travails of such an endeavor.

Suddenly she was at my side, taking my arm. "My lord has an appointment he dares not miss. We are very sorry for your loss." With that she steered me through the room and out into the front hall, so fast the butler found it needful to run to open the door before we collided with it.

The first few minutes in the carriage were agonizing and without speech. The sound of the wheels turning against the road had never seemed so loud. I opened my mouth to put an end to it, but it seemed Jane had conceived of the same notion.

"I cannot understand why you are so determined to undo yourself!" she huffed. "Your association with that girl has already caused trouble. Our visit was meant to prevent any rumors, not contribute to them."

"Yes, of course. You are correct." I stroked the scar at the corner of my mouth. "I am unable to see my way out of it, however."

"Out of what?" she demanded, her eyes wide with anger, her cheeks red. "You have not promised to do anything more for her, have you?" She narrowed her eyes at me. They shone like the most brilliant of emeralds. I had never thought her more beautiful.

"She has asked nothing. However, 'tis clear she expects some assistance in ascertaining who has killed her mother."

"Killed her mother? Whatever can you mean?" Jane looked scandalized. I knew her expression was merely a foreshadow of more to come, and from every circle of Society.

"It is perhaps merely her imagination, but she is persuaded that it was murder. Furthermore, she fears she is next."

Jane sat in stunned silence, followed by an urgent flow of words. "But who? And why? They haven't a penny to their names."

I sighed. "That is what I must find out."

"But you..." she sputtered. "You cannot mean..." She folded her arms across her chest, her gloves gathering up at her wrists. "I must insist you do no such thing!"

"How can I do otherwise? Who shall help her if I do not?" I did not add that it would, in some small way, atone for the fact that Willy had died the very morning I had arranged for his release from prison. If I did not assist her, Miss Andersen would be but one more bright light snuffed out too soon, like Willy, Johnny, Throckmorton...The thought of Miss Andersen's death added to theirs was more than I could bear.

"Julian," she said softly. She offered her hand for me to take. "I cannot promise Father shall overlook this fresh indiscretion."

"I am innocent of any wrongdoing!" I said more hotly than was warranted. I regretted it when I saw the flash of pain in her eyes.

"You needn't fear my loss of esteem," she said quietly. "I know the truth as well as you."

I grasped her fingers and, leaning forward, brought them to my lips. They were kid-soft in their leather covers and smelled of lavender and roses.

As I brought them to my cheek, my hand enclosing hers, she rose and reseated herself by my side. "Then we are agreed; there shall be no more seeking impossible answers, particularly on behalf of Miss Andersen."

I could not bring myself to speak the lie aloud. Instead, I wrapped my arms around her and kissed her so ardently that she could not fail to know the passion I felt for her.

Later that evening, after a long ride on my horse, I paced the floor of my chamber with a doggedness that prompted Jack to look in on me more than once. It was well past the wee hours of the morning when he brought me some hot milk, insisted I drink it, took the glass from my hand and pushed me onto the bed. Next, he tugged at my boots with such determination I could not help but cooperate. He tossed them into the corner of the room, (I had never come so close to dismissing him without a character) and blew out the candle without waiting for me to divest myself of my breeches. I realized he was either very tired, very annoyed, or both.

As he snapped shut the door behind him, I thought I heard a low chuckle. Deciding he was in too sour a mood to be amused, I fell asleep before I could wonder who had laughed, instead. It was a deep sleep, full of dreams.

I stood in the center of the dancing, Jane's hand in mine. The room was alive with color, music, excitement. I had my whole life ahead of me, full of all for which any man could desire. I was happy; happier than I could recall ever having been. It was then that I began to shake. Horrified, my hands dropped to my sides and my knees turned to water. Unable to name my ailment, I looked around for assistance. I nearly fell to the floor in a heap, but Jane took my arm.

"I am tired," she lied. "Let us find a place to sit." She drew me to the side of the room and through to an ante chamber reserved for ladies to rest in privacy. There were a few of such when we entered. I was only half aware of their presence, along with the dismay fixed to their faces when they looked into mine. As they scurried from the room, I fell into the nearest chair and took my head in my hands.

"What has happened? Julian?" Jane sounded apprehensive. No more than I. My reputation had been restored, I was one of the richest men in England, and I was betrothed to a beautiful woman who I felt certain loved me. Why, then, did I despair?

And then I realized; it was Willy. He had gone. It had been months since I had seen him; whether his ghost or a figment of my imagination, I could not say. He had died a year or more ago, but he had first left me when he had been thrown from his horse and was no longer himself.

It had been difficult to grieve his loss when he was still present in body, just as it was difficult to grieve his loss after he died. He had appeared to me so often since. In speaking with him in spirit, I learned he had been fully aware of all that passed after his accident despite his seeming idiocy. I realized it was not the accident, nor his *death that separated us–it was happiness. Mine. The pain seared through me as the tears sprang to my eyes. He was dead and I, for the first time in my life, was about to truly live. But how was I to live with myself?*

I woke the next day at an hour that would shame the most depraved of fellows. I rolled over onto my back, rubbed the haze from my eyes and, in disbelief, rubbed them again. Someone was standing at the curtained window, and it was not Jack. Nor was it Hatch. The figure was too trim to be, God forbid, Mrs. S., too tall to be any of the maids, and too short to be a footman. The only other person it could have been was the coachman.

"What do you want?" I groused. I was not accustomed to being bearded in my den by the stable hands.

"I only wish to help." The voice was mild, cultured, and almost as familiar as my own.

I bolted upright. "Willy?"

Laughing, he stepped from the shadows. "Who else?"

I restrained the desire to leap to my feet and throw my arms around him, as I had no wish to learn whether he was made of stern enough stuff to withstand my embrace. I could not bear it if he should prove to be merely a spirit. I preferred to think of him as alive...somewhere. Seeing him as he was, it was not the least difficult.

"What has kept you?" I demanded heartily, as if he had just returned from a ride about the park.

"Had I gone missing?" His smile was faint, as if he were as unsure of his query as the answer.

I stared at him, loath to ask a question that should prove he was anything other than alive. Whether I most dreaded that, or to discover that I was an addlepated idiot, I could not say. "Never mind, you are here now!" I was so glad to see him, despite my anxiety as to what it might mean.

"You passed a difficult night. There was much tossing and turning and twisting of the bedclothes," he said with a shake of his head. "What is troubling you this time?"

Perhaps he was merely the manifestation of my conscience. There were subjects upon which I could converse with none other; at least, no one I trusted as I did myself. "Jane is disappointed in me. I have a task to execute, one she cannot countenance. If I do not, however, I shall be the one who cannot look myself in the mirror again."

"With that phiz?" Willy scoffed good-naturedly. "I had thought you had left off mirror-gazing long ago."

I grunted in agreement. "You know of what I speak."

"Very well. What is this task?"

I had had many conversations with Willy since his death, but it had been nearly a year since our last. I moved past the strangeness of it and soon I had forgotten he lived in an alternate existence—if at all. "There is a young lady of little to no means, friends, or reputation. I cannot help but feel her pain as if it were my own. She is in danger, as well." I shook my head. "She is too beautiful to die."

Willy sat in his usual chair and pondered his response. "Do you admire her?"

"In the way I do Jane?" I pondered my own response for

a moment. "No, I do not." Now that it was said I felt relieved, as if I had been asking myself that very question from the moment I had first beheld the blue-eyed beauty.

"Are there any who might assist her in the manner she requires?"

I considered the possibilities. The cousin seemed detached from what was happening, her husband not much better. The doctor was a knowing one; too knowing. I realized I did not trust him in the least. Now that her mother was gone, that left no one. I said as much to Willy.

"It seems to me your path is clear. You must help this young woman."

"But what of Jane? She will not be happy. And her father shall be livid, I am sure of it."

Just then, Jack thrust himself into the room as if hoping to catch me at some misbehavior. I looked over at him in surprise—his face was cloudy.

"What is it?" I asked. "Say it is not Cook threatening to quit again."

He gave his head a brief shake. "There was talkin'."

I felt the heat rise in my face. I had never told Jack about Willy, nor did I think it wise. It was clear only I could see him. "I was having a conversation with myself, that is all," I said airily.

"Thot you stop't that." His expression was little short of a storm brewing.

I got out of bed and stretched. "Every man talks to himself on occasion. There is nothing odd in it." I flicked a glance at the chair and confirmed my suspicion. Willy was gone.

"I don't."

I chortled. "You speak to no one. You have said less than a dozen words in the past few minutes. I believe that is more than you have said to me in a month."

He said nothing in reply. I could have bet money he wouldn't have; I might have won fortunes. His expression of belligerence spoke volumes, however.

"Come along and help me dress. This room is freezing! Have you again told the maid not to disturb me by making a fire?" I said with disgust. "How is a fellow to walk upon his own floor?"

Jack scurried about, drawing the curtains, lighting the fire, pulling a suit of clothes from the press, dumping the dirty water from the washstand out the window. Meanwhile, I stayed out of his way as best I could and contemplated the improvement in my mood. I had not realized how much I had missed Willy. The very notion was cause for concern. Who misses being haunted? And yet, I did not feel haunted. Not today.

I hummed tunelessly as I dressed. I even endured Jack's insistence on tying the perfect cravat. He was far fussier about it than I, but I did nothing to dissuade him other than treating him to fits of impatience. I fixed my gaze upon the park in the center of the square and thought of how to go about learning who had killed Mrs. Andersen. There was also the puzzle of whether or not her husband had died by accident or through his own actions. I wondered if the two deaths could be related. And there was Miss Andersen's life to save. I could not have been happier.

Chapter Six

I descended to the breakfast room to find all had long been cleared away. Repairing to the salon, I pulled the bell and settled into the divan with the periodicals. I was well into a piece about the elephant that had walked upon the ice-hardened Thames during the Frost Fair when the paper was pulled from my hands. Standing with it between her fingers was Mrs. S.

I swallowed the rebuke that had sprung to my lips and took a deep breath. "How good it is to see you. How are you this morning?"

"It is the afternoon, and I have been resusticating over there," she said with a wave of her hand at a chair in the corner of the room, "for the best part of an hour."

Myriad questions came to mind. I settled on just one. "But why?"

She smiled like a cat that had bathed in cream. "I was persuaded you would wish to hear the latest *on-dit* as soon as may be."

Folding my hands in my lap, I prepared myself for the

diatribe to come. "And what would that be, my dear Mrs. S.?"

She gave me an arch look. "Might you not hypotherize?"

I stood to once again pull the bell. The sooner Hatch arrived, the sooner I might punish him for his negligence. "No," I said shortly. "It seems my hypotherizing skills are in want."

"How can that be? It all has to do with you and that Miss Andersen."

Her words propelled me out of my descent onto the divan. "I beg your pardon?" I asked, eyeing the decanters on the credenza.

"Only that you are somehow mixed up in the distinction of her mother."

"Extinction, er...by death of her mother," I corrected. That my thoughts would be better occupied absorbing the information she offered was, at the moment, a point too fine.

"Naturally, you must question the servants."

Inwardly, I winced. The questioning of the servants at Gilbert House had been unpleasant. Rey had been with me, then. He had helped to pass the time more pleasantly, but he currently resided in Barcelona with his bride, the former Miss Desdemona Woodmansey. It was a turn of events that no longer caused me the sorrow it once had. "They are bound to be a disapproving crowd," I hedged.

"Disapproving? The servants! Of you? How would they dare?"

"Servants dare far more than one realizes." I thought of Jack and his lack of temerity when it came to...just about everything. "In all fairness," I relented, "the servants I have had occasion to question are fearful they shall be falsely accused."

Mrs. S. gave me an arch look. "I am persuaded you would eschew false accusations with more acidousity than most."

"You are correct. Diligence in uncovering the truth has proven a higher priority for me than for the authorities." Had not Willy died of pneumonia whilst awaiting trial for a murder he did not commit?

"I see that you are hesitant," she said. "Allow me to accompany you!"

"'Tis a delightful prospect," I lied without qualm, "but you shall find it most tedious. The same questions asked again and again of one person after the next. 'Tis dreadfully dull."

"Very well, I shall trust your rendition and reserve tomorrow afternoon for your relatation of the pertinent information." She winked at me in a conspiratorial manner that made me wish to be gone immediately.

"I must apologize, Mrs. S.; I have rung twice and still we wait for our refreshment. I fear we shall wait forever. Perhaps you had best go home in anticipation of your visit tomorrow afternoon. Does that suit you?"

She nodded and went to the door just as it opened, revealing the butler who bore a tray laden with the answers to my most pressing troubles. She sailed past him, but not before snatching several bonbons from a plate on the tray as she went.

I intended to make the most of my meal; I knew little would be offered me by way of refreshment whilst I was occupied questioning the servants. Soon, however, I realized if I left immediately for Marlowe House, many of the servants would be conveniently between duties. With a sigh, I wiped the crumbs from my chin and set about informing the pertinent staff of my imminent departure.

The journey to Marlowe House was not long. I had nearly arrived before I recalled that Jane would be profoundly unhappy if she learned I had returned there. She had long made the restoration and protection of my reputation her personal pursuit. I could not deny that my choices affected her as much as they did me. It was an onerous burden to bear.

I rapped on the door anyway and soon I again found myself in the enormous salon with Lady Marlowe.

"My husband has taken Hannah out for a drive. She finds mourning too tedious, I fear."

I took in Lady Marlowe's ornate gown of black silk heavily adorned with jewelry of obsidian and deeply dyed lace and decided she had made a near-celebration of it. "Surely she is awash with grief over her mother's death," I suggested.

"But of course! Why should she not be?"

I thought I saw a challenge in her eyes that belied her

words. "That is a question worth asking, if you do not mind my doing so."

She shrugged. "The girl was thoroughly attached to her mother; there is no doubt of that. There is something about the physician that is odd, however."

I refrained from sharing my thoughts on the matter. "May I ask what you have been told as to the cause of Mrs. Andersen's death?"

"Not at all! She was never terribly strong. Our mothers were sisters and both of them died quite young, as well. I seem to be of a healthier constitution," she added with a smile that took years from her face. I realized for the first time that Mrs. Andersen had indeed been too young to die.

"Then it seems it was an unnatural death, an illness, perhaps. Was no malady ever named?"

"Not that I have been told. But, as I have said, she was always sickly. We were all overjoyed she survived carrying and delivering a child. 'Twas a blessing she lived long enough to see her daughter well on her way to being properly settled in life."

"She has you to thank for that," I pointed out.

Her expression softened. "And you. Though, whether she will have a season is yet to be seen. 'Twould not be in the least proper for her to go out so soon after her mother's death."

"She is as lovely as she is intelligent and has admirers already. I would not be surprised to learn Dr. Nuttall has considered making an offer for her, as well."

Perhaps I imagined it, but it seemed Lady Marlowe became agitated at my words. "He might make an offer, of course. Now that my cousin is gone, it shall be left to my husband to determine who should be given her hand." She sniffed. "Now that I think on it, such questions seem overfamiliar."

I realized she was correct and that it would not be easy to say what I had come to convey. "It is on account of Miss Andersen. I must determine if her mother's death was...unduly hastened in any way."

Lady Marlowe stared at me. "Why do you suppose it is any business of yours?" she demanded.

"It is not a duty I undertake of my own accord, I assure you. I believe it shall not betray Miss Andersen's trust to reveal her wish that I discover the truth behind her mother's death."

"As to that," Lady Marlowe said matter-of-factly, "I should be astonished if she did."

"I am persuaded it was not your intention to assume me a liar," I said gently. "Perhaps there is another reason that you doubt my words."

She looked down into the inky depths of her lap. "Her mother was ill for many years; there can be no doubt of that. If Hannah has asked you to look into it, I must assume she only does so that you shall dance attendance on her."

I lifted my quizzing glass to my eye. "I am persuaded you are mistaken," I retorted. "Each time we have met, I have been in the company of the lady I am to marry. She knows very well that my path is set."

"So was that of Dr. Nuttall's when they encountered one another. Not a day has gone by that he has not been in the Andersens' company since!"

"Dr. Nuttall was meant to marry?" When Lady Marlowe nodded, I dared to pose another question. "Do you think him attached to Miss Andersen? I had thought him far more interested in her mother until I saw how he stood guard over her the last time I was here."

"He is attached to her, indeed." She vented a gusty sigh. "Whether he sees her more as daughter or wife, I cannot say."

"Lady Marlowe," I said slowly, "I do depend upon your opinion. I am a stranger to your family; however, my decision to offer financial support to Miss Andersen, for the sake of her fallen father, has put me in the center of things. She seems to regard me as someone she can turn to in trouble. I find I cannot deny her request. But, am I right to say you believe her to be inventing a story merely to gain my attention?"

"Have I not said so?" she asked in tones of irritation. "She has always behaved as if the world ought to revolve around her. You might assume my cousin spoiled her; perhaps she did. As an only child and often her mother's sole companion, it is not difficult to imagine how it has happened. She is, as you say, a lovely girl. Perhaps she is right to believe having everyone wrapped around her finger is her due."

I thought Lady Marlowe most likely correct and likely

resentful, as well. "Your husband: how does he feel about Miss Andersen?"

Lady Marlowe stood, her chin held high, her hands twisted in a knot. "I do not believe it is any of your concern. Now, I have an obligation to be elsewhere. Banner shall show you out."

With that, she pulled the bell and quit the room. As I had never been invited to sit, I was not obliged to jump to my feet with her abrupt rising. However, I had not had the chance to ask permission to question the servants. As I was certain she would have denied me such, I decided it was no significant loss. I allowed myself to be shown out the door by the silent Banner. My heels against the floor rang louder than ever before.

I found myself standing on the stoop with no companion to assist me, no ideas of my own, and no options. I felt utterly alone, and yet the sensation of being watched gradually impinged upon my mind. The notion grew such that I began to feel some apprehension. Perhaps Mrs. Andersen *had* been murdered, and the one responsible had me in sight. I restrained a shudder just as I felt a tug at my sleeve. My heart jolted as I turned to face my attacker, fists swinging.

I nearly took Jack's nose off, but he was quicker than I and ducked. Before I could congratulate him, chastise him, or collapse into him in relief, he again took hold of my sleeve and dragged me down the area steps. Memories of traversing the same steps at the home of a murderer, only to find the disfigured body of a girl I had failed to save, rose heavily in my mind. "Now what have you done?" I cried as my feet were dragged through a puddle of murky water that had collected at the landing just outside the kitchen door.

Ignoring me, as he was wont to do, he knocked and slipped into the shadows behind me. I hadn't a moment to react before the door was opened by a stout woman with the usual girdle of keys about her waist. Reminding myself that I had before been in this same position, I opened my mouth to inform her of my identity, but nothing came out.

"Yer a Runner!" Jack hissed from the depths of darkness at my rear.

I was just about to insist I was not a Bow Street Runner when I realized my quest should prove easier if I claimed to be one. "Good day, madam. I am Clotworthy of Bow Street."

"La!" the housekeeper squawked, her eyes round with fear. "Wot has 'appened?"

I hadn't any idea what to say, especially once I realized I was dressed too fine for an agent of the law.

It was once again Jack who kept his head. "Ask yer questions," he hissed.

"Indeed," I said with a vulgar clearing of my throat. "I am not here to take anyone away," I assured her, though she looked anything but. "I needs must ask a few questions." When the woman stared at me, her mouth open, I cast about for something that would convince her. "'Twould be best if you were to let me in."

Wordlessly, she stepped aside. I entered with only a slight pang of misgiving for Jack who would be left behind just as more rain began to fall. "Thank you, Mrs...."

"Brown. Wot are yer questions, sir?"

"I have a great many questions to pose to a great many people; all of the servants, in fact. Would it be too much trouble to provide me a small room where I might speak with each in private?"

To my delight, she nodded and led me to her sitting room deep in the bowels of the basement level. Pleased with my success, I decided to press it. "And I shall require tea and cakes."

"O'course," she said, entirely nonplussed. She showed me into a room unexpectedly small and dank in comparison with Sir Thomas' obvious wealth. However, the chair by the fire was generously proportioned and richly padded. I sank into it gratefully and prepared myself to wait.

Mrs. Brown quickly returned with the promised pot of tea and jam tarts so thick with the sticky spread, my mouth watered. Feeling it more practical to make the most of this unexpected repast before asking off-putting questions, I ate and drank my fill. "How long have you been in service to the Marlowes?" I asked with the last swallow of tea still warm in my mouth.

"Sixteen years."

"And have you known Mrs. Andersen for all that time?"

She shook her head. "Never 'afore laid eyes on 'er. This is the first she 'as come to London."

"But there are other servants in the house who have waited on her, is that not so?"

"Yes," she said firmly, her expression a combination of curiosity, wariness, and a deep integrity.

"I should very much like to speak with all the servants who came in contact with her, as well as those who waited upon Miss Andersen and Dr. Nuttall."

"I suppose it shan't hurt any," she muttered as she rose and quit the room.

It was clear she knew nothing of any value. I waited with anticipation for the arrival of whomever she sent. The young girl who next entered the room was an abigail; a lady's maid. Though I had never, for obvious reasons, employed such a creature, I had learned much about servants of all types during my quest to exonerate Willy Gilbert.

"Good afternoon," I greeted her. "Is there anything you can tell me about Mrs. Andersen, her daughter, or her physician?"

The maid's brow furrowed. "Wot kind o'things?"

"Anything unusual. No detail is too small."

What followed was a litany of mundane information of which I had never before been so unfortunate to hear. Finally, I interceded. "Has there been anything unusual in the behavior of those three people? Anything that struck you as odd?"

"Now tha' you say so," she said, seating herself and leaning across the table in a conspiratorial manner, "I think the sawbones to be very odd. He has naught to do with leechin' or bleedin'. I have been in the room when he has laid his hands on various parts of the lady's, er, well..."

"Body?" I provided.

She nodded, her eyes wide. "And then he would mumble some words. I ha' never seen anythin' like it. The daughter never seemed like she thought it at all strange. But it is said they come from Africa so p'raps they are used to strangeness."

"Indeed. What else has been said of them?" I found I was much better accepted as an agent of the law. The servants seemed to feel more comfortable with a man who was not of the nobility. I made a mental note of the information and forged on. "Has there been any gossip?"

"Oh, but o'course. There is always gossip 'bout the owners of a house. It is said that the Miss is too full of herself. She wants to be treated like nobility even though she ain't."

"Does she have any suitors? Has anyone sent her flowers or called on her?"

"I wouldn't know," she said, drawing herself up. "I am a lady's maid and don't cope with the flowers or visitors, sir. But, I was often in Mrs. A's chamber when the doctor came to call. The both of 'em brightened up considerable when he arrived."

"I see. Have you observed the doctor's reaction? Do you believe he preferred one over the other?"

"I couldn't say, but he has been stayin' in the house since before the mother died. If he had come just to see 'er then he ought to have moved on, oughtn't he?"

"Perhaps he remains as Miss Andersen's physician. Or her particular friend."

"I han't seen him give her any med'cines or mumble over her like he did the mother, if that is what you mean."

"Medicine. Did he leave much of that for Mrs. Andersen?"

"Oh, yes! The only one allowed to give it to 'er was him or the daughter."

I recalled the whiteness of Mrs. Andersen's face the night of the ball and wondered if she might have been poisoned. "Could anyone else have obtained a bottle of something? Either one he had left, or one from his bag when he was perhaps not attending to it?"

"Who would do such a thing? And why? There was never no one in the room wif us—just the ladies, the physician, and me."

"Were you always present when he was in the room?"

"Well, no, I suppose not."

"Then you cannot rightly say someone else was not there when you were not present."

"Uh, well, yes—some other maid might 'ave been in the room when I weren't. Bu' none of us would have wanted the lady dead. We ain't killers, sir!"

"No, of course you are not. If I were to return, would you be willing to answer more of my questions?"

She nodded, and I asked her name. "I be Marybeth, sir."

"Very good. If I return, I shall ask for you most

particularly. Now, will you send in the downstairs maid so that I might ask her about flowers?"

"O'course," she said softly, with a shy smile. She turned to look at me over her shoulder just before she shut the door. I thought she rather liked me. It surprised as much as it delighted me.

The person who entered the room next was not, however, a maid. It was Banner, the butler. "My lord!" he cried. "What is this?"

"Nothing," I said as I rose to my feet and went to the door. "If you have anything to tell me about the goings-on here, you may find me at Silvester House in Grosvenor Square."

I left him staring after me, his mouth hanging open. I feared 'twould be difficult to ever regain the confidence of the staff at Marlowe House.

Chapter Seven

"Jack!" I called when I had climbed the stairs to street level.

He appeared at my side, his clothes plastered to his skin by the rain, his teeth chattering. To my regret, I was furious with him. I, a peer of the realm, had professed to be someone I was not. To be found out was humiliating. The Marlowes' butler and housekeeper were likely crowing about it over a pot of tea of their own. And Jane would not like it, of that I was certain. She was already not fond of Jack, and now he had put me in a most awkward position.

It was clear he was not above telling tales or encouraging others to do so. Suddenly I could think of nothing but my cousin's ring—the one he had given me and which I had lost. Perhaps Jack had taken it, after all. He looked up at me, a question in his eyes.

"Find that ring!" I shouted as if it had been he, not Hatch, I had charged with its recovery. I then strode away so fast he had to run to keep up. He gave up after half a block and allowed himself to fall increasingly farther behind. It infuriated me anew; I realized he would not have gained the front steps of Silvester House as I mounted the stairs to my room in want of a hot bath. A full hour later, as I slipped into the heated water, I began to question everything I thought I knew about the boot boy. I had rarely felt so low.

Despite my misgivings, I allowed him to select my suit for dinner at the Leavitts'. I watched his every step, sometimes baldly, though mostly surreptitiously. I had trusted him too completely, I could see that now. What else he might have stolen and most likely pawned was limited only by the number of possessions not currently under my purview. How long had it been since I had perused the valuable books in my study, or asked Hatch for an accounting of the silver plate?

Jack seemed to sense something was wrong, which only irritated me further. "That is quite enough of that!" I barked.

"Wot? Wot 'ave I done?" he demanded in a manner thoroughly unsatisfactory.

"You are skulking about the room like a dog with its tail between its legs. Which reminds me; I must put a question to you." I turned from viewing my ensemble in the mirror to face him. "How did you know I was on my way to Marlowe House?"

"It's me bizness," he muttered, his gaze skittering from mine.

My suspicions mounted. "What exactly is this business?"

He looked up and directly into my eyes. "To know yer bizness, that's wot!"

77

I was too astonished to be angry. "And how do you arrive at such knowledge?"

"That's wot I'm sayin'; it's me job to know." He very nearly glared at me but remembered himself just in time.

"I do not recall informing you, or anyone for that matter, of my intention to question the servants at Marlowe House. How did you know of it? Answer me!"

He looked down at the floor, hesitating.

"Well?" I demanded.

"Y'said it, like you were tellin' someone 'bout it."

My conversation with Willy flooded into my memory. "Oh. Well, as I have said, I am a very good listener." We stared at each other for a moment, his defensiveness apparent in every line of his body. "Go tell Hatch I shall require my carriage."

He left without a word. It was not unusual, but I thought I saw a new defiance in his eyes. I could not trust myself to judge accurately when it came to the boot boy, however. How I longed for someone to speak to about it.

"I am here."

It was Willy. "By Jove, 'tis good to see you!" I exclaimed. "I have had the most exasperating day."

He spread wide his hands. "I am here," he repeated.

"Yes, you are. It seems you always turn up when I am feeling my worst. 'Tis not a coincidence, is it?"

He frowned. "I couldn't say. I am simply...here."

A question I had feared to ask sprang to my lips. "Always? You are never...elsewhere?"

"Where else would I be?"

I laughed despite my disappointment. I longed to ask where he went when I was not present. He would most likely answer my question with one of his own. "I do not suppose you know where my ring has gone missing, do you?" It was but a jest, though he did not seem to realize it.

"I seem to recall hearing it bang against something; perhaps the chest of drawers."

I got down on my knees and swept my hand under the piece of furniture. Fetched up against one of the back legs was something hard, round, and cold. I drew it out with amazement. "How long has it been there?"

"How long has it been missing?"

I was not amused. Sighing, I chose to abandon such questions. "I have treated Jack poorly. Everything was finally right, and then..."

"Then?" he prompted.

"Then you turned up," I murmured.

"Are you certain that is how it happened?"

"But of course! I was glad to see you."

"When was that?" he asked, his expression unreadable.

"Do you not remember? You commented on what a bad night I had passed."

He smiled, but there was no censure in it. He was invariably kind.

"I suppose I was already feeling some distress before you arrived." I turned the ring over and over in my fingers and pondered my choices. "Jack is no ordinary servant. He is, I suppose, a friend of sorts. He is extremely loyal. How wrong it was of me to accuse him."

"Falsely," Willy added.

"Yes. How dreadful he must feel!"

"As dreadful as do you?" Willy asked.

"I think not. The pain of regret is much like a blade." Who could know the truth of that better than I? "How could I have believed him to have stolen anything from me?"

"You made a mistake. As such, you feel as if your honor has been tarnished. There are few things in life that distress you more."

"Who would not be distressed by such?" I began to pace the room, anger welling. "Who has been forced to endure the tarnishing of my honor more than I?"

"You have had to endure much, Trev," he said gravely.

This admission of my pain somehow lessened it. Better yet, I found I could now think of someone other than myself. "And you. You have had to endure much, as well. After the accident, you were excoriated for your deficits in riding, when everyone knows you were the best horseman in the county. You were thought weak-minded and treated like a child; worse, an animal, by those who knew nothing about you. Even those who loved you and knew you best assumed you were less than you were. It must have been insufferable!"

"It taught me a good deal of patience," he said softly. "There were times when I wished I were dead. Most days, though, were better. I learned to find pleasure in small things. I was often left alone with my thoughts—much as now."

I marveled at him, how he smiled in the midst of his solitude. "Willy, I...I do not know what to say. I wish I could put an end to your grief. But know this—I am delighted you are here, and that we may speak together as we did when we were boys."

Willy smiled. "I enjoy it, as well. Mostly. You can be a trifle rattle-pated!"

I laughed at his old jibe for me. "I go to the Leavitts' tonight. I shall see Jane and then I will feel better."

"Shall you tell her of what you learned today?"

"About the Andersens? I think not. She is not in favor of my investigations. She fears it shall unnerve her father and he shall never allow us to marry."

"And what of you? Do you not fear the same?"

"Yes," I started then hesitated. "Was it not you," I said slowly, "who insisted I must help Miss Andersen?"

"Did I? I suppose you must have agreed it to be a good notion or you would not have embarked upon it."

I knew he was right, but the conversation left me with an unsettled sensation in the pit of my stomach. "Well, I am off to dinner." I turned to collect my coat, hat, and gloves. When I opened my mouth to bid him goodnight, he was gone. I took care to shut the door softly behind me anyway.

I spent the journey to Jane's home in thought about Jack. How did one apologize to one's servant? I was clearly in the wrong, and both of us knew it. Perhaps I could make it up to him in some way other than an outright admission of guilt. That, however, would make him as uncomfortable as it would me. No, I needed to land upon something small and indirect, such as a visit to the tavern for a meat pie.

Now that I had settled on reparation for Jack, I turned my thoughts to how I might continue to grant Miss Andersen's request without vexing Jane for not honoring hers. Turning the matter over in my mind, I looked at it from Jane's point of view. I realized it must appear to her as if I had a *tendre* for Miss Andersen. That would never do.

By the time I was ushered into the drawing room of Leavitt House, I had resolved to give up Miss Hannah Andersen and the questions of her parents' deaths. 'Twas not worth alienating Jane. In truth, I was not likely to discover anything pertinent to the facts. When I saw how Jane's face lit up when she saw me, I knew I had made the right choice.

Dinner was the usual over-extravagant affair I had come to expect at the Leavitts'. The table groaned under the weight of far too many choices; one could never hope to sample all. Seated around such bounty were Walter and Jane on one side, with Mr. and Mrs. Leavitt at either end. I was seated next to an elderly aunt I had occasion to meet once before. She was pleasant enough but refrained from strong opinions on any subject, making her a desultory conversationalist. Her brother, Mr. Leavitt, was quite the opposite. His uncompromising opinions on all and sundry were served up with the food in an endless round of tedium that nearly made me wish I had chosen to wed another.

"And whilst we are speaking of upstarts, one cannot fail to mention Sir Thomas and his wife!"

My glance flew to Jane, who shook her head very slightly.

"I believe we have heard enough on that subject," Mrs. Leavitt said with a nervous twitter.

"He is but a baron!" her husband roared as if such a circumstance excused his condemnation. "If he had a noble bearing or were his baronetcy older than the day is long, one might hope to tolerate his behavior. But to go about with a crest on his carriage...it's heavy-handed, that's what it is!"

"I believe it is his right to display his crest on his carriage, my love," Mrs. Leavitt soothed.

"How does such a man acquire a crest when I, one of the richest men in England, have none? It's a travesty; that is what!"

"Papa, perhaps we might speak of something else, at least whilst Lord Trevelin is with us."

Mr. Leavitt lifted his gaze from his plate to stare at me, his eyes narrowed, and his lips turned down. "I suppose you have a crest to your carriage, too."

I nodded. "The crest belonging to the Marquis of Trevelin is an old one, dating back to..." I began, but he cut me off.

"I am certain it is a fine crest! You needn't harp on it as if 'tis a dispensation from the king!"

"Actually, it is a dispensation," I said, but was again interrupted.

"If we are to change the subject, and I say that we shall, let it be to speak of that cousin of theirs—Miss Andersen. She is the most deplorable of them all. If my daughter were to ape her betters in such a manner, I would have her horse-whipped."

I looked to Jane in alarm and was glad to see she did not appear to be in the least frightened. "Of course, you would not, Papa. You spoil me far too much, you know you do."

"And you allow it, young lady!" he said, pointing his fish-laden fork at her. "It is unbecoming in anyone, let alone my daughter! You had best watch yourself, for I meant every word. The horsewhip is always to hand!"

"Yes, Papa," Jane murmured.

His angry disapproval made my stomach churn and I found I could no longer eat. What's more, it distressed me to see Jane so treated. I told her as much when we had a few moments alone together on the divan. Her father and brother had lingered long over the port in the dining room, but I excused myself with the ladies. Mrs. Leavitt sat in the corner of the drawing room with a bit of embroidery, too far away to make much of our whispers.

"We must marry soon, if only to remove you from this house!" I insisted.

"You know as well as I that Papa is mostly bluster. Still," Jane mused, her brilliant green eyes flashing in the fire of the nearby hearth. "I wonder if that is true when it comes to Miss Andersen. I have doubts that he is the only one to view her so uncharitably. As for myself, I am mortified by his behavior tonight. I pray you excuse him."

Smiling, I put my hand over hers where it rested on the damask between us. "I would do anything for you; even give up my quest to discover the truth behind Mrs. Andersen's death."

Jane was so silent at this revelation I began to wonder if she had misheard me. "In truth," she finally said, "I believe I have more compassion for Miss Andersen than I first did. Indeed, she does behave as if she has a fine title and a large dowry, but I find it no longer troubles me. She is now an orphan and alone in the world save Sir Thomas and Lady Marlowe. They mean well, I am certain, but their influence is not very large in Society."

"I tend to agree." I ran my thumb along the smooth flesh of her hand, delighted she had chosen to refrain from donning her gloves after supper. "I do not know, however, what I might do about it."

"You might do as she has asked." She looked eagerly up into my face. "You may help her discover if her life is in danger. The poor girl; 'twould be dreadful if she were to be killed as well!"

Taken aback, I chose my words carefully. "So, you wish me to continue to aid her, despite your father's obvious prejudice against the residents of Marlowe House?"

"Yes!" She put a hand to my face, the side where dwelt the scar. "But be careful. And discreet. I have no wish for Papa to learn of it."

I opened my mouth to speak, but she put her finger to my lips. "Wait. I have something I must tell you." Her face glowed like a pearl in the sun. "Papa has agreed to a summer wedding!"

Chapter Eight

I rode home feeling as if I could fly. I went immediately to bed with plans to rise earlier than was my habit, so as to call on Miss Andersen as soon as possible. Willy did not manifest in order to offer his opinion on the matter. It was just as well; I had little doubt as to the wisdom of my actions. Jane and I were in accord with what should be done, and that was enough.

I presented myself at the door of Marlowe House the next morning, having entirely forgotten the previous afternoon's encounter with the butler below stairs. The expression on his face when he discovered me standing on the stoop was without price.

I had no choice but to brave it out. "Is Miss Andersen at home?" I asked, adopting my most proper expression.

He opened his mouth and closed it again several times before he finally intoned, "Whom shall I say is calling?"

I was likely the only marquis to have entered that house, but it was not the moment to quibble. Rather, I presented him with my card, which gained me entrance. I was invited to wait in a much smaller chamber than the one in which I had previously met the occupants of the house. It suited me very well, as it was more conducive to a conversation of any illumination.

Miss Andersen took her time in arriving. That she was most likely not expecting visitors so early in the day was a fact I had failed to consider. I wondered if she believed it fashionable to make me wait but dismissed the thought as uncharitable. When she did appear she looked nearly perfect, in a simple, white silk gown, with a standing ruffled collar that brushed against her chin. It seemed much time had been spent on her hair, but the overall effect was spoiled by evidence that she had been weeping.

"Miss Andersen," I cried, jumping to my feet. "What is it? How can I be of service?"

She sat and waved for me to do the same. 'Twas somewhat galling to be treated as an inferior rather than given my due, but I brushed my annoyance aside. Though I would not have tolerated such treatment from nearly anyone else, she was new to town, and had been raised in trying circumstances. As such, she required my patience. I began to perceive, however, why Jane's father had accused Miss Andersen of aping her betters.

"I am afraid there is nothing to be done," she said bluntly. "My mother is no more; it cannot be remedied."

"And this is what has already provoked such sorrow this morning?" I asked kindly.

She nodded, her face drawn downwards with grief. "She

was my mother, yes, but also my staunchest friend and constant companion." She dabbed her eyes with a handkerchief. "I miss her most dreadfully."

"Yes, of course you do." I, too, had lost my mother at a young age. A decade had passed since, but not a day had gone by that I had not thought of her.

She looked up with a smile, forcibly bright. "Please excuse my lack of mourning," she said with a glance down at her alabaster gown. "Lady Marlowe arranged for the mantua-maker to come to the house and fit me out in the proper attire, but nothing is yet complete. I am afraid I arrived in London with no black. I wore so much of it after the death of my father that I have refused to wear it since. So many sad memories," she said, her lip trembling.

"It is only I; you need not fear my disapproval. I shall expect the bills for your mourning clothes to be sent to me, as well." The words were out before I could regret them. I felt the perspiration start up on my brow.

"Thank you." She plied the handkerchief a trifle more assiduously than before. "I did not know what else to do. Lady Marlowe has not taken a liking to me, you see, and Sir Thomas is afraid to go against her."

Unsure as to how to respond to such a revelation, I elected to change the subject. "I have been pondering your fears as to the cause of your mother's death. Do you yet feel as if you are in danger?"

"Oh! Please say you have come to help!" she cried in tones almost joyful. "You cannot know how much I have suffered, believing her life was cut short—as mine could be, as well. It is dreadful; I trust no one!"

"Not even your cousin?" I asked in astonishment.

Her face darkened. "As I have said, she has not taken a liking to me."

"You cannot think she means to murder you! Besides, she liked your mother well enough, did she not?" Miss Andersen nodded in response. "If you believe someone has deprived your mother of her life and this person wishes to do the same to you, how can it be Lady Marlowe?"

She looked struck. "I suppose you are correct. I had suspected her, but now that I think about it, I do not believe she would have willingly killed my mother."

"Very good. We have eliminated one person. Now, what of Sir Thomas?"

Miss Andersen sighed. "He is a spineless creature. I believe he likes me better than he lets on, but either way he could never resolve to take such an action."

"Excellent! That brings us to either Dr. Nuttall or one of the servants."

She gazed at me, her expression a mixture of alarm and regret. "Do you truly suspect him? I am persuaded Mother should never have allowed him in the house if she thought him dangerous."

"Of course, she did not," I hastened to assure her. "That does not make him any less so."

"Then you *do* think he did it?"

"Let us first define what 'it' is," I suggested.

She offered what I can only describe as a *moue*. (What it was meant to convey, I could not guess.) "It is murder, of course. Is that not what you came to discuss?"

"The possibility, yes. More importantly, I came to ensure your safety. If your mother's death was aided by another, we must prevent the same from happening to you. But first, we must determine the reason anyone should wish your mother dead."

Tears filled her eyes. "I cannot think of any! That is the trouble. Who should want to kill her? She was already so sickly. She has been at death's door many times. I cannot imagine why whoever it was could not wait for nature to take its course!"

I put my hand to my chin but refrained from stroking the scar, an action I often took when deep in thought. "May I ask from what ailment your mother suffered?"

She sighed, gustily. "What did she *not* suffer? Her inability to have more children after I was born, the death of her husband, the insistence from all who knew us that we were not worth their esteem. Then there's the poverty, no doubt hunger—she denied herself so that I would have enough to eat. She was a good and dutiful mother, and a generous friend. She had no enemies that I know of, and it is the truth!"

I was pained by her distress and regretted that I had need to pose more questions. "It is clear you think highly of your mother, Miss Andersen. I'm afraid there is nothing in that to help, however. What of Dr. Nuttall? He is a more recent acquaintance, is he not?"

She pinned me with an arch glare. "My lord, that is quite inequitable of you. To assume he is wicked only because he is somewhat mysterious is unjust!"

I smiled, rather grimly I expect. "In what way is he mysterious?"

She smiled back, far too gaily. "I believe it was your word, my lord; an accurate one, indeed. It would take far less time to list the ways in which he is not."

Though I did not recall having referred to the physician as mysterious, I nodded my desire to hear this list.

"Very well. He hails from Groomsbridge in Kent, no children, is a widower—'tis a sad story; best not to speak of it. He is clearly a man of means if one were to take notice of his wardrobe. He is well educated, highly intelligent, and uncommonly handsome."

It was all I could do to refrain from laughing outright; her observations of the man were so clearly motivated by the romantic sensibilities of a young maiden. "If it is true that he attended Magdalene College at Oxford, he possesses an enviable education."

"I believe he subscribes to various theories of healing, including something he refers to as homeopathy."

"A German practice, from what I understand," I mused.

"I would not know. But he does not limit his treatments to the theories of one country; he utilizes practices from India, China, and Scandinavia, as well."

Silently, I wondered which country to attribute for the chanting the maid described. "What of English practices? Does he prescribe medicines approved of in this country?"

"Oh, yes! Mama experienced a great deal of pain, the cause of which could not be determined. For that he prescribed laudanum, mercury, and arsenic."

"None are out of the ordinary." I knew, however, that all could be fatal if too much was taken. "However, none of them should be administered over-frequently."

"He always leaves the strictest of instructions," she insisted.

"I am certain he does." I gave her a reassuring smile. "It is, however, a means through which someone might have killed her. If indeed someone did," I hastened to add.

"What do you mean?" She frowned. "They are medicines."

"True, but there are many substances one can imbibe that will cause harm if not used correctly."

Her face paled. "Do you believe Dr. Nuttall prescribed too much?"

"If he is a poor physician, yes. In which case, your mother might have died of misadventure. Either way, the authorities should be alerted."

Her gaze flew to my face. "I have no wish to see him jailed for an accident!"

It was obvious she was half in love with the man, but it would not do to withhold the truth from her. "How are we to protect his future patients otherwise?"

She opened her mouth to speak then seemed to change her mind. Rising to her feet, she gestured I should remain as I was and went to stand by the hearth, her back to me. I could only assume she needed to give vent to her feelings and had no wish for a witness.

Her feelings overcame her, however, and she began to weep in earnest. Reminding myself that it was as she wished, I was powerless to help. Nor could I blame her; how bitter to believe her mother might have died due to the medicine meant to cure her.

Finally, she spoke. "Why?" she wailed. "Why have I lost both my father and mother through such tragic means?"

'Twas a predicament with which I was most familiar. I could not remain seated in the face of such sorrow. Rising, I went to her side and placed a hand on her shoulder. To my astonishment she turned and crumpled against my chest. Deeming it best that she cry it out, I put my arms around her. It was not in the least romantic. I could think of only two things: the wretched state of her feelings and that of my cravat when she had done with it. When the storm abated, I put my hands to her shoulders and gently extricated her from the once-snowy linen.

Her expression was more wistful than aggrieved. "What is so sinful about being poor? My father died. My mother has always been ill, and we were all alone. Why do people assume it was an act of evil that brought us to this state?"

"Is it your fear you shall again be treated shabbily because of how your mother died?"

She nodded. "It is more than that, however. Others feel justified in judging the unfortunate. I suppose they believe the poor have earned their fate through their own choices."

"Perhaps there are those who do," I allowed. "Though, I have oft observed that to be visibly poor is to confront others with their lack of charity."

"Do you truly think so?" She stepped away and, wiping her eyes, returned to her chair. "How arrogant." She sighed. "It is more malicious than that, however. The rumors of my father's death... it is as if Society believes our poverty to be our punishment for no reason save that my father chose to die. But he did not! I am sure of it! And neither did my mother."

Her words prompted in me a new thought. "Do you suppose there are those who will assume your mother took more medicine than she was meant to in order to end her suffering?"

"Of course! Such misapprehensions have been known to happen."

I knew this to be true. "Did she have access to the medications?" It pained me to ask, but I had to know whether Miss Andersen was safe from a potential killer.

"I administered all of her medicines. When she was near the end, I was with her day and night. The last time we were separated was when I ran from the room the night of the ball. Do you recall?"

I nodded. "So, if you were with her from then until she

breathed her last, you must know she did not choose to take more medicine than she ought."

"That is correct! But it shall not stop the gossips from saying their worst." Her voice was drenched in despair.

"I regret to say we must again consider the possibility that someone acted to end her life. But, may I ask? If your mother was so sick, why not accept it was simply her time to die?"

She seemed the picture of indecision; her lips pressed tightly together, her eyes narrowed. Finally, she spoke. "I do not know. I suppose she had been the same for so long. And then, quite suddenly, she grew very much worse. It was too sudden. Would it not appear unnatural to you?"

"I take your meaning," I said, my heart sinking. "I believe it best if I leave you now. But first, would you share with me your thoughts on your father's death? It seems far-fetched, but there is a possibility the two might be connected."

"Yes, I see why you ask," she said with a faint smile. "I was quite young, and though I have asked Mama many questions she did not seem to have the answers." She drew a deep breath. "It was an unexpected attack by the Xhosa; the natives. My mother and father were in constant dread such a thing would happen. I believe they had a plan that if such should occur, my father would get us out of harm's way. Of course, he meant to return to do his duty. But first, he wanted us to have a chance to escape."

She swallowed hard, as if to push back the terror. "I

remember we were driving along a road at an alarming rate. To one side was the face of the mountain, and the other was the edge of a cliff. The conveyance we were in—some sort of cart with one horse—lost a wheel and we went down very hard. Father was thrown right over the side. He managed to hold onto the edge of the cliff, but it was too much—he slipped and fell to his death before help could arrive. I do not know that anyone would have known where to look for us. All of the men were fighting."

I recalled Mrs. S. had insisted Miss Andersen had attempted to rescue him. I hesitated to ask her about it; however, she must hate herself for having failed. "And you and your mother were, naturally, not strong enough to attempt to pull him to safety?"

She looked down at her hands, the wad of handkerchief too wet to be of any use, and shook her head. "She was attempting to attach a rope to the horse to aid in his rescue when he..."

"How agonizing for you." I swallowed the lump that threatened to rise in my throat. "I have no wish to further distress you, but how did you get to safety? Did you walk back to civilization? And what of your father? Was his body ever recovered?"

"Mama, as you may imagine, did not know what to do. She feared we would be punished for Father's choice to get us away. We remained where we were until a white man—I do not know who—met us on the road and conveyed us back to the garrison." Her chin quivered as more tears poured down her face. "I do not know how Father's body was collected. It was such a long way down."

It was a dreadful story, but I forced myself to push on. "I beg your pardon most humbly, Miss Andersen, but I must ask: where was your father buried? I had thought to go to Africa to solve the riddle of his death, but perhaps he is not there," I suggested.

"There is no need to go to Cape Town!" Her eyes were wide with alarm. "There is nothing left of the Andersens there."

"Then he rests in peace here in England?"

"Yes," she said slowly, as if it were difficult to call the memory to mind. "We brought him home on the ship. He is buried at our parish church in Ashford, Kent.

"In a family plot?" I wished to know if he had perhaps been buried outside consecrated ground with those who had taken their own lives. It would say much as to how his death was viewed by others at the time.

She seemed affronted. "Yes, of course! Where else would he be?"

I realized she had no concept of how suicides were treated. It was a detail I understood to be too distressing for so young a mind. I determined to learn where he was buried for myself. It seemed the logical place to start in discovering the truth behind the deaths of Miss Andersen's parents.

"Thank you," I said, rising. "I promise to discover what I can. In the meantime, please be careful. Naturally, your cousin shall want to keep you close. I cannot advise you as to the safety of Dr. Nuttall, but I ask you to take care. Do not imbibe anything he might wish to give you. Eat and drink only what others are in the house. Do you understand?"

"Yes," she said eagerly. "I shall do exactly as you say, my lord."

I inclined my head in departure, but she failed to rise and perform the customary curtsy. I wondered if she were entirely ignorant of the customs, or if she so wished to be seen as having risen above her station that she refused to behave properly.

The next morning, I along with Jack, climbed aboard my obnoxiously crested carriage and made for Ashford.

Chapter Nine

The following afternoon I stepped out into the hushed, wintry confines of the graveyard at the village church. Rows of intricately carved tombstones glowed in the light of the setting sun. Beyond them, the naked branches of monumental oak trees pierced the sky, relinquishing bits of accumulated snow in cadence with the frigid breeze. Just past the stand of trees stood an arch of ancient stones that bridged a chuckling stream. At either end was a clump of rose bushes under a light dusting of snow. It was nothing short of utterly peaceful, but Jack refused to venture out of the church.

As the clerk was at his dinner, it would be some time before the records could be accessed. I began to inspect the tombstones on my own. Jack emerged just as I came to the end of a long row some distance from the church door. He whistled a wavering tune, his hands jammed in his pockets. To his evident dismay the sun chose that moment to fall below the ridge of a hill, and the graveyard was plunged into shadow. I sent him back to fetch one of the lighted torches from the iron grate on the wall inside the church. He returned quickly and by the light of the flame I started on the next row of stones. I walked slowly, reading the names, resisting the urge to take in the full story of each. Jack, nervous, followed along behind.

I pretended not to notice. "We shall stop to get meat pies at the inn before we turn in for the night," I promised by way of encouragement. In the dark, it was difficult to catch the gleam of appreciation in his eye. "If you were to fetch a second torch, we could be there all the sooner."

Jack's expression of dismay resembled a macabre glare in the leap of the flame.

'Twas then I recalled he could not read. "My apologies, Jack. Perhaps you would be so good as to return to the church and learn whether the curate has finished his supper."

Jack bolted away and disappeared into the building faster than I had thought possible. When I turned to continue my work, I noticed that the stones were not as tidy as they had been closer to the church. Dead weeds poked up through the thin layer of snow, while the stones demonstrated a preference to slant this way or that, leaning one upon the other like drunkards on their way home from the tavern. The thought made me smile. Suddenly I realized I now searched a section of the graveyard that was far too old to contain the remains of Mr. Andersen. With a curse, I began to retrace my steps, when a blow was landed on the back of my head with such force that I lost consciousness.

I was wakened by Jack and the curate, a torch in his hand. Mine was lying snuffed out beside me in the snowy grass. The evening had deepened into night; it must have taken some time for them to find me in the dark. I sat up and immediately regretted it. Sinking down into the loam, I groaned my pain.

Jack fell to his knees at my side and ran his hands through my hair, pressing his fingers along my scalp.

I yelped when he found what he was looking for. "That hurts!" I said tartly.

He said nothing, but his breath was ragged as he wiped his fingers on his breeches.

Somewhat alarmed, I put a hand to the spot that pained me the most. My fingers came away sticky with blood. I cleaned them in the freezing grass and began to feel around for my hat. Some notion that dwelt in the murky mists of my mind led me to believe donning it was vital to my respectability.

Jack jumped up and found where it had rolled behind a tombstone, helped me to sit up, and placed it on my head. Sitting upright was not as painful as it had been the first time, but I noticed I felt dizzier. "Help me up, man," I directed the curate, and between the two of them they managed to get me to my feet. As the three of us made our way to the church door, I staggered back and forth like a drunken tombstone along the dark green river lined with egg-shaped boats on either side of us, three Knights of the Round Table.

To my abject wonder we entered an underwater grotto strewn with sparkling jewels. Magma-induced fire sprang from cracks in the surface of magenta and amber-colored rocks whilst the song of a musical river accompanied us as we made our way out of the double doors and into the velvet night. A pair of seahorses tethered to a glowing yellow conch shell stood in wait and I was helped aboard. Jack took the reins and the slap of the chill breeze in my face brought me back to reality.

"We mustn't forget about the meat pies," I said and was rewarded when Jack's lips twisted into something resembling a smile. As I laughed at this extravagant show of emotion, my head exploded in a shower of stars. They went out all at once and I knew no more.

I woke to the sun shining through the drapery at the window of my room. I looked to see if Willy waited for me in his customary chair. Only, 'twas not Willy; 'twas Jack. And 'twas not my room. Rather it was mine at the inn we had stayed at the night prior to visiting the...I could not remember where. I attempted to sit up and immediately regretted my decision. "Chamber pot!" I ground out before launching what was left in my stomach over the edge of the bed.

Jack had anticipated such a reaction, however, and neatly caught the worst of it in a basin. The remainder hit the wood floor with a splash.

I put a hand to my head and groaned. "How long?"

"One night."

"So, we were at the church yesterday afternoon?"

Jack nodded.

Gingerly I slid into a seated position. "Did you see who did it?"

"No."

I had thought not. "It could have been anyone, for any reason. However, it is safe to assume someone wished to prevent me from learning the answers I was seeking. If so, it must have been someone associated with Miss Andersen."

Jack gave no sign he was listening. He had finished cleaning the floor, had dumped the chamber pot out the window, and was now rinsing it with water from the basin.

My stomach grumbled. "Go below and bespeak me some breakfast."

He glared at me, doubtless opposed to the possibility of more soiled floors, but went away as instructed. He had barely left when the door again opened.

"You!" I cried, astonished to see Dr. Nuttall.

"Yes." He looked at the floor as if ashamed. "'Twas I who landed that blow to your head."

I eyed him, warily. "And now you have returned to put a proper end to me?"

"I have come," he said, his voice quiet, but firm, "to ensure I have done you no lasting harm."

"How good of you!" I quipped as I adjusted my position to one of more comfort (and, if I am honest, more dignity). "Are you to tell me why?" I was apprehensive, even frightened, but preferred he not learn of it.

He turned as if to depart, hesitated, then pulled up a chair and sat. "It was on account of Miss Andersen. I very much wish to protect her."

"And how am I a danger to her? I am working in aid of her, or did she not tell you?"

He gazed at me, his expression frank. "She did not. Somehow she learned you had pelted off to find her father's grave. The notion upset her. I cannot say why."

"And so you struck me?" I was every bit as incredulous as I was without doubt. "*You*, a physician?" (And I a nobleman!) "What did you use, a cricket bat?" Gingerly I probed the egg-shaped mound on the back of my head.

He frowned. "Truly, I must beg your pardon. It was not well done of me. I thought only to prevent you."

"What harm could possibly come from locating her father's place of rest?" I asked in exasperation.

"I cannot say. Perhaps the answer lies in the reason you came in search of it."

I had wished to know if he had been buried in the family plot. It was only then I realized I ought to have begun with the area to which the suicides were banished. "I am not at liberty to disclose such information."

He stood. "Very well, then. Again, I deeply regret the ill I have done you. Might I suggest you indulge in a good meal?"

I stared at him, appalled. "You are acting as my physician now?"

His normally somber face cracked into a smile. I saw

then the youthful charm to which Mrs. Andersen had doubtless been so drawn. "It is my duty."

I was in no mood for such levity. "My servant shall soon return. I must advise you to be well away from here by then. He is as jealous of me as you are of Miss Andersen," I said, flicking petulantly at the counterpane.

His smile vanished. "Yes, of course. I shall be happy to wait on you in London, should you feel the need to further discuss the matter."

I scowled at him, unable to formulate a tolerable reply.

With a nod, he turned and quit the room.

I sighed with relief. He had tried to stop me; that was reason enough for my anxiety, and yet I had never trusted him. I thought about what Miss Andersen had said about Dr. Nuttall. He was a widower—a sad story was associated with his circumstances. A voice in my head (it sounded eerily like Willy's) pointed out that most widowers have a sad story to relate. Miss Andersen reported that the physician hailed from Groomsbridge near Tunbridge Wells. I decided to journey there to learn what I could.

When Jack returned, the innkeeper staggering along behind with his tray of piping-hot food, my stomach growled in appreciation. Once I had put down most of it, I announced our immediate departure for the east.

His mouth fell open in protest. "Bu', I mus' git ye 'ome!"

"I realize how difficult it is to desert the delights of a London winter for the miseries of the country," I said wryly.

He stared at me, his expression belligerent. And yet, the manner in which he worried his bottom lip with his teeth led me to believe he was more anxious than rebellious.

"Come, come," I insisted around a mouthful of toast. "All shall be well. It's not the first time I've had my pate caved in." A vision of Willy, his brain injured, his arm withered, and his smile twisted out of shape, rose into my mind. It was a thought too far, and I once again cast up my accounts. Wiping my mouth with a cloth, I conceded defeat. "Very well, then. We shall remain until my stomach can be persuaded to behave."

He walked away wordless, as was his habit, but I thought there was a swagger to his step I had never had occasion to witness.

It was not until the following morning that we headed for Groomsbridge. The weather was milder than that of London, and we soaked in every ray of sunshine we encountered. We stopped first to partake of a light luncheon at the inn, then proceeded to the parish church. Jack stayed behind with the carriage whilst I went inside and requested information about the Nuttall family. The curate was most helpful and soon we were on our way to Nuttall Cottage, a sprawling country house on the edge of the village. Upon our arrival I signaled the driver to stop and rolled down the glass.

Jack jumped down from his seat on the box and gawked at the splendor. It was a grand house, hundreds of years old, with graceful mullioned windows and a roofline punctuated with gothic arches. It sat up on a hill quite a distance from the high rock wall that bordered it. It was approachable only through a wrought-iron gate.

"I had not realized he was so well-off," I mused, gazing at the house through the carriage window. "Even so, his story is tragic." Jack said nothing in reply, but I knew he was listening. "His wife disappeared and has never been seen or heard from since. He was out of the country and returned to find her gone." I registered his expression of woe from the corner of my eye as I descended from the carriage. "He never learned what happened to her. They had been married less than a year."

His sniffling was audible as we walked up to the heavy iron gate. Its hinges promised to be the sort that creaked. For all appearances, it had been some time since the house was lived in. There was doubtless a caretaker about the premises, and I had no wish to be seen. "Perhaps we had best return after dark."

Jack lost no time in racing back to the carriage. He opened the door for me and hurtled up onto the box for the return journey to the village and its accommodations. I had suspected him to be of the superstitious sort, but I had not realized how deeply it ran. I could only hope the house would be no more forbidding at night than it was during the day.

In this I was greatly disappointed. Its large windows and pointed arches that were pleasant enough in the light now seemed positively sinister. Jack followed behind me so closely I fancied I could feel his breath on my neck.

"Tis all right," I said in response to his wordless terror. "Merely refrain from making noise and no one shall be aware of our presence."

"How're we t'see?" he griped.

"We have the moon," I said, checking the sky for clouds, "though you shall need to locate the tinder box once we gain the house." I rested my hand against the cold metal of the gate and ever so slightly pushed. The squeak it emitted was faint, but it did not budge. I turned to consult Jack on the matter, but he was gone. It took all of my self-restraint not to shout his name. I told myself not to panic and was rewarded by the sight of his face—on the other side of the iron grille, the key to the gate in his hand.

"Wot?" His smile as he opened the gate was decidedly cheeky.

"How?" I hissed as I crept past him.

He pointed at an opening in the wall, very low to the ground and so small even a bloodhound would have trouble making its way through. I resolved to instruct Cook to feed Jack better as I led the way to the front door of the house. What I hoped to find inside was a question I had not yet attempted to answer.

Chapter Ten

It was again through the offices of Jack's slender frame that we gained entry to the house. He crawled through a window that had been left slightly ajar, prompting me to reconsider my decision to fatten him up; he was decidedly useful as he was. We stood in the front hall whilst our eyes adjusted to the lack of moonlight. "There," I said, pointing through an open doorway to a room with a large hearth visible in the light of an enormous window.

He was quickly gone and back again, tinder box in hand. Nothing occurred to indicate he had experienced the least difficulty in finding it; he seemed to have an instinct for such things. For the first time I wondered if he had led a life of crime before joining the Canning household. I then dismissed the question as a moot point; I could never betray him, even if it were to satisfy justice.

"Jolly good," I whispered as I went about the business of creating fire. He brought me a taper from the candelabra by the door and soon we stood in its glow. More doors that led into various reception rooms met our gaze, and in the center of the hall a staircase, most of which lay in a pool of the deepest shadow.

I hadn't the least wish to ascend them. They brought to mind a frightening encounter on a staircase whilst investigating the death of Johnny Gilbert. And yet, something inside me insisted what I sought was ever upward. With an intake of air that was both gasp of fear and surge of courage, I began to climb.

To my disappointment there was naught that seemed untoward, despite my apprehension. As I didn't know what it was I looked for, nothing proclaimed itself as being of interest. Unlike the grounds the house had an air of life, as if its master were merely in the next room. Though I knew he was not, the notion flooded my mouth with saliva. I swallowed hard and proceeded along the first-floor passage.

"Wot're we lookin' for?" Jack whispered.

I jumped with fright; I had forgotten his presence entirely. "Quiet!" I insisted.

He mumbled something so softly I could not make it out. My mind was too occupied with why I was drawn to the highest portion of the house. 'Twas an attic room in which a suspect in the Gilbert tragedy took his life right before my eyes. I repressed a shudder at the thought. Looking about me I saw that there was nothing but more reception rooms on this floor, including a cavernous ballroom. I headed up to the second.

As expected, this floor was nothing but bedchambers. The room that was most likely Dr. Nuttall's was wood-paneled, abundantly adorned, and free of dust. Next to it was a more feminine chamber. The walls were covered with a shimmering fabric in the same shade of blue as a robin's egg. It deemed further consideration; the room where his wife had slept promised to provide clues to the state of their marriage.

First to claim my attention was the dressing table. It was littered with dozens of expensive, white wax stubs that seemed to glow in the moonlight that streamed through the window. I lowered my taper to ignite their wicks, wrinkling my nose as the stench of scorched dust rose into the air.

Revealed in the light of the flames were various pictures propped up against the black-draped mirror. Brushing them free of cobwebs, I discovered that each depicted the same young woman. One was a portrait in the tradition of Reynolds, very fine. There was also a less-adept sketch in pencil, a miniature enclosed in glass, and a watercolor painting.

I was both astonished and stirred when Jack took the miniature in one hand and held it to the light. Together we bent over the image with its chestnut curls, rich sweep of lashes along a curved cheek, and brown eyes, bottomless as a cup of chocolate. Mrs. Nuttall was a beauty. With a low whistle he carefully, almost reverently, returned it to its place.

I must confess I felt rather envious I had not had the opportunity to meet her. Turning away, I took in the other features of the room. The bedframe was resplendent with silk drapery, the windows the same. Various objects were laid out on the coverlet as if in wait for their owner: a dust-covered night rail, a hairbrush decadent with cobwebs, and a mob cap flattened by its own layer of gray. A gown that looked to be pale rose under the grime was tossed onto a bright blue chair, its color still easily perceived through the dust.

There was also a writing desk, a delicate, fine-boned chair, and a large clothespress. Its door stood ajar, failing to confine the deluge of dresses that tumbled out of it. I stroked the one nearest to hand; it felt alive against my skin as if accustomed to such treatment. Indeed, it looked as if someone caressed them regularly; they bore very little dust compared to the other items in the room.

Suddenly, I became overwhelmed by a sense of unease. 'Twas as if we stood on holy ground upon which we had no right to trespass. This woman—this wife—was much loved, of that I was certain. "Come," I barked far too loudly. "We are done here."

Jack helped me to snuff the candles that had not sputtered out on their own. I was about to take the stairs downwards to quit the house entirely, but there came a loud crash from below. Turning, I dashed silently upwards, careful to keep the candle alight. Eventually I found myself at the door of a bare, unfinished room at the top of the house.

I slipped inside, Jack my shadow, and closed the door. He stood with his ear to it, listening and breathing too heavily, I daresay, to hear anything else. I looked about the room; it was empty. The walls were unfinished, as was the floor. I had to take care not to put my foot through the plaster of the ceiling below as I moved about. Its state was at odds with the rest of the house with its highly polished floors and rich, painted walls.

As I held the taper aloft, I caught sight of something in the darkest corner. It seemed out of place. Carefully, I drew close enough to determine it was but a scrap of fabric, white and ghostly, that clung to an exposed nail in a wall beam. It was nearly at the level of the floor. I wondered who had crouched so far down to have caught his or her clothing on it. I held the flame closer and noticed a space between where the beams of the wall and the floor ought to have met. It was not large and appeared to have been created by floor beams that had rotted away.

"Jack," I hissed. With a wave of my hand, I held the candle such that he had enough light to pick his way across the treacherous floor. "See if you can fit your hand through here," I instructed.

He skipped from one floor beam to the next until he was by my side and studied the hole. Casting me a look of doubt he got down on his knees, one to a beam, and thrust his hand into the pitch-black cavity. "S'deep," he grunted. He leaned forward, and the hole swallowed his arm up to the elbow.

It was then that a loud crack came from the passage. Heart pounding, I turned to face whatever danger threatened us. I peered into the darkness, but there was nothing visible. The sound was not repeated, and it seemed we were safe for the moment. I turned my candle to shine again upon Jack just in time to see his feet disappear through the floor.

"Jack!" I called wildly, peering into the cavity. My cry was followed by a clamorous rattling that moved swiftly downwards. 'Twas not until I heard a thud followed by a troubling silence that I realized he had fallen, head first, through the gap to the floor below. "Jack!" I cried, again and again, as I bolted from the room, flew down the stairs, and fumbled about along the second-floor passageway.

It was dark, my candle having blown out, but I followed the sound of the screaming. To my astonishment I spotted a faint light. It tallied with the direction from which came Jack's wails. I ran towards it as fast as I dared in the dark, spotting the edge of an open door just before I collided with it. Throwing it aside, I raced into the room. Instead of Jack, however, I found a large man with a lantern, too absorbed with the mound at his feet to give me any notice. I, too, stared at it as I ran, attempting to make sense of the bundle of fabric, sticks, and splintered beams.

Dropping to my knees, I slid across the polished floor to the now-silent heap. "Jack!" I cried as I pawed through the pile. I was crazy with fear, my heart pounding faster and faster. Alas, every handful was only white muslin and lace, rotted flooring, and sticks of smooth wood. Suddenly Jack burst from the pile, a matted wig in his hand. He stared at it

115

in horror, and with an abject cry of terror, threw it across the room. It hit the floor with an unexpected *thunk* and rolled to a stop, exposing three black hollows that seemed to stare up at the ceiling.

"Aaaahh!" I howled as I leapt to my feet. Jack chose the same moment to catapult himself into my arms, his own around my neck. He was sobbing, his tears hot against my skin, mumbling unintelligibly.

And then the man with the lantern spoke. "So, that's wot 'appened to 'er!"

Jack fell instantly silent, snapped shut his mouth, and relinquished his hold on my neck. Thrusting himself away from me, he tripped over his own feet and hit the floor mere inches from the hairy ball. With another blood-curdling scream, he hurtled out the door and down the stairs at a dead run.

The large man and I took one another's measure, the pounding of my heart in tandem with Jack's descending footsteps the only sounds.

"Who're you?" the man finally demanded, his words slurred with drink.

I did not hesitate for a moment. "Clotworthy of Bow Street." I spoke in courageous tones that belied the lurching of my stomach at the sight of the sad heap. It was now clear that the smooth pieces of wood I had picked up and cast aside were actually bones—human ones.

The man shifted his gaze from me to the pile at his feet. He leaned closer with the lantern, his eyes fixed to what looked to be a small white stone. The very air in the room seemed to still as I gazed at what I realized was the skull of an impossibly tiny babe. With dawning horror, I unquestionably knew this pile of refuse to be the remains of the beautiful woman whose image I had just admired, and of her unborn child.

My head felt light and my stomach began to heave. I needed an urgent departure. "'Twas clearly an accident of some sort," I said in my best imitation of a Bow Street Runner. Then I bolted from the room and down the stairs to the ground floor, and out the double doors at the front of the house.

I deposited my dinner in some shrubbery and looked around for Jack. Calling for him, I dragged fresh air into my lungs as I made for the gate. I was quick about it, certain the man with the lantern was after me. I took no care to ensure the gate did not screech as I went through and arrived at the carriage just as Jack opened the door. "Go!" I shouted for the coachman as Jack and I threw ourselves inside and collapsed against the velvet squabs.

He sat huddled on the seat across from me, his eyes wide, his knees tucked under his chin. There had been a time, not many days prior, that I had believed him unafraid of anything. I now knew differently, starting with his fear of tombstones at the church, but had no wish to avail him of my reassessment of his character.

"I suppose we may remove Dr. Nuttall from our list of suspected killers," I said in the calmest tones I could manage.

"Wot?!" he cried, his face red and the veins of his neck purple. "He kil't her!"

I frowned. "'Twas clearly an accident. She must have trod on the floorboards and broken through, much as you did. If the fall did not kill her outright then she remained there, unable to free herself, to die of thirst and starvation," I added, unwisely. "'Tis horrible to contemplate!"

"No! He kil't 'er and put 'er there!" He rubbed savagely at the tears on his face.

"Dr. Nuttall was out of the country," I reminded him.

"Says who?" he demanded. "E'en so, he migh' 'ave come back and no one the wiser."

I was forced to admit he could be correct. Exhausted, I gingerly lay my sore head against the cushions and considered. "I suppose if he wanted her dead he could have returned and done the deed, slipped the body into the cavity, and left again, as you suggest, without seeing anyone. If so, it was cleverly done. No one has thought him guilty."

Jack nodded, his chin wobbling as his eyes filled with fresh tears. "An' she so beau'ifu'!"

"Indeed, she was. And, in my estimation, well-loved. She was also with child," I said thoughtlessly.

"He kil't her *and* his babe?" he shouted, his hands knotted at his sides.

"It would seem so," I mused, wondering what manner of man would do such a thing. He loved her, of that I was certain. He ought to have loved his child, as well. "Perhaps he returned home and found her too far gone with child for it to be his. It might have been an accident. A moment of rage. Or perhaps he suddenly no longer cared what happened to her."

Jack glared at me, then turned his face into the high, buttoned, velvet of the seat and said no more.

I rapped on the ceiling of the carriage and instructed the driver to stop at a tavern, any tavern, the sooner the better. I had no wish to eat ever again, but I owed Jack some meat pies. He had fallen asleep and did not wake even when the carriage drew to a halt. I prodded him in the shoulder and immediately rolled down the glass to speak to the coachman. When I turned around, I caught him rubbing his eyes. Instantly, he dropped his hands and pretended to look for his hat.

I, in turn, pretended not to notice. "It seems the groom is hungry. I believe I shall go inside and determine if there is anything worthy to be had."

Jack followed me out of the carriage and stayed close rather than take himself off to wherever it is that servants eat their meals. I bespoke three meat pies and a bottle of something to drink before making myself comfortable in the private taproom, the one set apart for gentlemen. He knew better than to sit at my table. Rather, he stood in a far corner of the room, deep in the shadows until the food arrived. Once the waiter had left Jack ran to the table, scooped up a pie, and devoured most of it before he had returned to his corner.

"Come, come," I insisted. "We are alone. I have no

wish to dine at the present and there are yet two pies to be eaten."

He did not need to be told twice, but still refused to sit. He shifted from one foot to the other in a sort of dance as he did away with the remaining food.

"Well, that was hardly worth removing from the coach for," I teased him. I pulled out a coin and bade him bespeak a small sweetmeat for himself. His eyes lit up as he reached for the blunt. With a sigh, I watched him go. I thought that perhaps he would soon be restored to his old fearless self, after all.

Soon afterwards, a gentleman in a bottle-green coat and spectacles entered the room. I watched him for some time in an attempt to get the measure of him. Was he a local? A traveler? Anyone who could tell me anything about Dr. Nuttall and his ill-fated wife? I noticed his supper was meager, consisting of a board of bread and cheese and a tankard of ale.

When he had finished dining, I rose. "Do come and share my bottle." I held it aloft, and with a broad smile he joined me.

"Good evening; I am Mr. Brough." His accent was northerly, perhaps even Scottish.

"And I am Mr. Silvester," I said in modest tones meant to discourage questions. I had no wish to reveal myself as a marquis. "Tell me if I am wrong, but I believe you have traveled far to be here."

He smiled, his pink cheeks rising to meet the roll of

flesh beneath his bright blue eyes. "I have, but it was long ago. I am a resident of Groomsbridge."

Delighted, I poured him a generous glass. "Originally from Scotland, then?"

He took it with a nod and drank it down in one gulp. "Indeed, but years since past."

I decided against posing as an authority from Bow Street and chose a different profession. "I write for the periodicals; gossip and local scandal, et cetera. I refuse to go so far as to draw cartoons," I added with a wry smile. "Nothing that clever, but just as interesting I hope. If you were to share with me the tales you have heard in the area, I could see my way to paying you in coin."

His eyes grew wide and his smile wider. "Capital! 'Tis capital, indeed," he insisted. "I should not like to say anything that might upset the lady wife," he said with a sudden furrowing of his brow. "But let me see, I must come up with something that would not make her deplorable amongst her friends."

"No, that would not do." I gave him my fullest smile, the one that made the scar seem to disappear.

"You a married man, then?" he asked with a chuckle.

"I am soon to be, and very fortunate indeed. I do know, however, what it is to stir up trouble amongst one's peers. I would not take it amiss should you change your mind." I was prepared to be disappointed, but just as hopeful that the Broughs removed to Groomsbridge after Mrs. Nuttall met her tragic end.

"Well, let us see," he mused, running his fingers along his chin. "Many interesting things have happened here in the village, but they all involve people whose opinions we value. You understand," he said with a nod. "But there is one tale I feel no compunction in sharing."

My spirits soared and not because of the drink.

"There's a physician hereabouts who calls himself Dr. Nuttall."

I raised my brows in mock surprise. "Is he not a doctor, then?"

"One cannot say for certain. He has patients enough. They don't die at a rate faster than any other's. No, his story is more personal."

I took up my glass and leaned back against the wooden settle. "Then he is no friend of yours. Might I ask why?"

"'Tis no secret, no indeed. The man is a mountebank! I would sooner have the school master in to dine than Mr. Nuttall."

"I see. (I did not.) Then he *is* a sham?"

He frowned. "Of sorts. It is said his wife disappeared whilst he was out of the country. But everyone knows he did away with her!"

Chapter Eleven

This was the sort of talk I had hoped to hear. "If he has killed her, how has he remained a free man? Or is he?" I added, remembering in the nick of time that this was the first I had heard of one Dr. Nuttall.

"He is free, indeed! Presently, I believe him to be practicing in London."

"How can this be?" I asked, setting my glass on the table and leaning close.

"The poor lady was never found," he said with a wink and a finger to his nose.

A memory of the lady in question with all of its macabre images rose into my mind. I hadn't the luxury, however, for sentimentality. "Ah! Then his guilt would be questionable." I poured him another drink. "I think, though, that you believe him to be guilty."

"Well, yes, I do," he said, a trifle petulantly. "I don't like the man! He is odd. He has traveled to strange places. He leaves his house locked up for long periods of time."

His words triggered in me a fresh notion. "Perhaps he

loved his wife and cannot bear to reside where they lived so happily together."

"Perhaps," he said judiciously. "That being said, the village are somewhat divided on the matter. There are those who think he killed her and disposed of the body, and those who call on him for his services." He shrugged.

"I take it that you and your social circle are of the former opinion."

"Indeed," he said with a quaff from his glass.

"I thank you. 'Tis an interesting story, to be sure," I said, reaching into my pocket for a sovereign and sliding it towards him.

It was his turn to lean in close; so close that our noses nearly touched. "When you write the story," he said in a low voice as he placed his hand over the coin, "do be sure to use the man's initials. 'Dr. N'. You see?"

"But of course," I assured him. "'Tis a scandal sheet. We always use initials." And yet, the use of such a device had done nothing to protect my reputation when my story had been written up in the periodicals over two years prior.

"Well," he said, rising. "'Twas good to meet you, Mr. Silvester. I must be on my way, however. The wife, you know. Indeed, you shall know soon enough!" He tipped his hat to me and headed for the door, his gait only slightly tipsier than it had been when he arrived.

I sat half in shadow, half in firelight, lost in thought. It seemed a portent that the village were as divided about the innocence of Dr. Nuttall as were Jack and myself. However, I found I could not dwell long on such things. Instead, my mind would not refrain from wandering to Mr. Brough's parting words. I wished to know what he meant about his wife. I wished to know how it applied to my future with my wife, as well. My Jane. How would life change when I had her to go home to each night?"

My mood mellowed with the wine and daydreams of her in my bed. As I slid lower on the bench, I suspected the mornings should prove just as delightful as the nights.

Miss Leavitt and I stood together at Vauxhall Gardens under a canopy of exploding, colored lights. The fireworks were spectacular, particularly from our position in the Dark Walk, an area of high hedges that afforded a man and the object of his affection a semblance of privacy.

Behind this screen of greenery, I itched to hold her. My neck had a crick in it from looking up into the sky and my arms felt like logs dangling at my sides. I suspected they would feel far more like themselves if wrapped around Miss Leavitt. Slowly, I placed my hand on the center of her back. The fabric of her gown was smooth, and my gloved hand slid over it like a skate on ice as she turned to face me. She looked up at me with delightful anticipation. Our gazes entangled until mine strayed and became firmly locked on her mouth.

I quickly realized that, despite her lack of height, if I put my arms around her I could easily lift her lips to mine. I only hesitated for a moment; she had never given me cause to believe she would be repulsed by the sensation of my scarred mouth on hers. Eager but gentle, I pulled her close and kissed her, lightly at first. When she

125

put her arms around my neck and leaned against me, I became bolder. She ought to have rebuffed me. Instead, she returned my ardor. It felt as if she offered me her whole self, body and soul.

There had never been a moment as sweet.

'Twould be heaven, I knew, to wake up to such a face; far more preferable to that of Willy's.

I jerked upright, my mellow mood flown. How would I speak with Willy when Jane was in the room? Would I wish to? Would he go? If he stayed, to what private moments would he be privy? The notion caused me no undue amount of alarm. What's more, I did not want Jane to think I spoke aloud when alone. It was bad enough for Jack to think so, but Jane? No! I could not bear it. She was too intelligent. She might think me mad. Perhaps I even was.

Jack chose that moment to open the door of the taproom and peer inside. He had found something else to do whilst I entertained the man in the bottle-green coat but was now ready to retire. He invited himself to ride inside the carriage again, an impertinence I chose to ignore, and together we fought off yawns on the drive back to our inn. Neither of us mentioned Mrs. Nuttall or her tiny child. As best as I can recall, we never spoke of it again.

Willy and I, however, had a lengthy conversation about the physician the morning after we returned to London. I suppose I, as usual, did most of the talking. Willy was, as always, an excellent listener.

"How am I to prove he did it? That is the question," I averred.

"Hmmm, yes, indeed," Willy replied.

"You sound skeptical."

"Not at all; I am merely unsure of his guilt." His smile was apologetic. "But if you have reason to doubt his innocence, I feel certain there is cause."

"That is of no use," I protested.

"Nevertheless, it is my wish to help. Perhaps you ought to tell me more."

I threw my hands into the air. "I have told you everything I know."

"There is doubtless more to learn. I know you, Trev; you shall get to the bottom of it."

There came a scratch at the door and I turned to see Jack, his expression part accusation and part apprehension. Quickly I turned toward Willy's favorite chair. He was gone.

"I said that *I* shall get to the bottom of it. However, Jack, I think it shall be the both of us who solve this mystery."

His expression softened, and he went about helping me with my morning toilette. As he removed a suitable ensemble from the clothespress, I contemplated my plans to call on Dr. Nuttall to question him about my discovery. I laughed to myself, shaking my head, when I recalled Willy had instructed me to learn more about the matter. He needn't have prodded me.

Jack had returned to his taciturn ways upon our return from the south, but I caught the reflection of his scowl in the mirror. He held the jacket of blue superfine up to my chin whilst I pretended to give it a great deal of scrutiny. I would not have chosen any differently, but I wished to allow him a victory.

"That will do," I finally conceded. "Bring me my jewel case." I wished to look my most imposing for my interview with Dr. Nuttall.

Jack did as I requested, and I rooted around in it whilst he attempted to strip me of my nightshirt. I selected a large Topaz stickpin to make the most of the canary-yellow waistcoat Jack had selected. It seemed fitting to add the large gold signet ring to my ensemble. I held it in my hand, its cold weight heavy against the flesh of my palm, feeling it warm until I could no longer feel it at all.

I cracked open the wax seal of the letter that had accompanied the small parcel Hatch had brought me. It was Eve's seal, the one with the large, scrolled double R that he affixed to all of his correspondence. I was greatly surprised; the two of us had been out carousing only the night before. He claimed the evening to be in celebration of my recovery from the injury done me in the duel in which he had saved my life. Whatever he thought it important to say to me, or give me, he could have done so many times already.

Dear Trev,

Weeks have gone by since the duel and I have not thanked you for risking your life to save mine. As your cousin, I shall always be a part of your family. However, I wish to make you a part of mine—the Rogers-Reimann family. As such I give to you my signet ring, the one with which I shall seal this very missive. Wear it always to remind you of your bravery and the love you bear me. And I you.

Yours, Evelyn Rogers-Reimann

I opened the parcel to find the gold signet ring. I had been so preoccupied by the notion that he had jumped in to save my life when Rutherford attacked I had forgotten why he had done so. I had done the same—had gone against the rules of dueling to save Eve from the duke's frenzied charge. I realized there would have been no need to save my life if I had not first saved his.

I slipped the ring onto my finger, but it was far too big. Eve wore it on his smallest, and yet it was still too large for my ring finger. I changed it to my index finger and was satisfied. I felt it a very fine gift, indeed.

Now that Eve and I had parted company, I still had a fondness for the ring. I felt ashamed of my belief that Jack had stolen it from me and felt the heat of it along my neck. I glanced at him, his patience strained, as I came out of my reverie and allowed him to continue with his work.

When all had been completed to his exacting standards, I regarded the results in the mirror. Save the scar, I thought I had never looked finer. I instructed him to have my things waiting below for my departure immediately following breakfast. It was shockingly early for morning calls, but I wished to speak to the physician before the ladies of the house were up and about.

The sky was clear and blue as I stood outside of Sir Thomas' townhouse, but it was cold enough for my breath to frost the air. Purposefully I strode to the front door, determined to be admitted entrance, whilst castigating myself for my indecisiveness. I was a marquis! And yet, I was young. More than that, the memory of my temporary ostracizing still pinched. Who was I to accuse a man of murdering his dearly loved wife? I drew a deep breath and rapped on the door.

It seemed the butler was yet entertained by pulling a face of surprise whenever he saw me. I ignored him and stepped inside before he had a chance to speak, my many-caped greatcoat swirling in the air as I turned to confront him in the front hall.

"I wish to speak to Dr. Nuttall immediately. It is a matter of some urgency."

Banner went away without a word and I was left to stand in the hall like a commoner. I saw that the door to the room in which I had conversed with Miss Andersen was open. Putting the tip of my cane to it, I gave it a gentle nudge. It opened wide enough for me to determine that the room was empty, despite a merry fire burning in the grate. I entered and divested myself of my coat, hat, and gloves which I placed with my cane on the table by the door rather than having them taken from me by the butler, as was proper.

Choosing the most imposing chair in the room, I waited in its cozy depths until Dr. Nuttall appeared in the front hall. "In here," I said pleasantly enough, considering the man could very well be a killer. Could very well have been *my* killer that day in the graveyard.

"My lord!" he cried as he stood upon the threshold and looked about. "I am pleased to find you well."

I offered him a smile that left one in doubt of exactly what it was I felt. I found it excessively useful, as far as smiles went. "Please sit down. There is much to discuss."

His face drained white but he sat in the nearest chair, one which I ensured to be low and uncomfortable.

"I have recently returned from Groomsbridge." It seemed to me he turned paler at my words.

"Groomsbridge!" he exclaimed. "I had thought you in Ashford."

"Indeed, that is where I was when landed that blow," I said, with a lift of my hand to the offended spot at the back of my head. "But I went on from there."

"But why?" he asked, seemingly puzzled.

"To learn more about you. Is that not where you lived with your wife?" I thought I would have trouble even speaking the words that alluded to that poor, unfortunate woman, but in that I was mistaken.

His spine seemed to stiffen, and his head jerked back in surprise. "My wife? What do you know of her?"

His surprise seemed so sincere that words nearly deserted me. "I regret to inform you," I said, my voice thickened by the lump in my throat, "that your wife's remains have been found."

His face went from white to fully red. "Remains?" He leapt to his feet and went to stand with his back to me at the fireplace, just as Miss Andersen had the week prior. He propped his elbows on the mantel and put his face in his hands. "She is dead, then."

I suddenly realized I had no proof, no authority to verify the truth of my words. We had fled the scene without notifying the authorities. I felt every bit as much a criminal as if I were her killer.

"I was there. At the house. We...I discovered her body. She had been wedged in the wall of the attic, but her remains, they have...fallen. What is left of her now lies on the floor below."

He turned to stare at me, his face an unreadable mask. "But how? How did she die?"

I shook my head and swallowed hard against the lump in my throat. "Either she slipped through a hole in the floor of the attic, or someone placed her there, alive or dead; it is impossible to know. She has remained there, caught, all these years. 'Twas most likely the bulk of the babe that kept her suspended between one floor and the next."

His eyes grew wide and the lines around his mouth tightened. "My wife had no child."

I drew a deep breath, knowing full well my words might come as a blow. "The child was not in her arms when she fell. She was expecting one." I felt the pain that flared in his eyes as if my own. Hastily, I looked away, but heard as he returned to the chair and collapsed into it.

"My wife died in a wall, where the child I never knew she carried prevented her from gaining her freedom? She has been there for all this time? All these years?"

As he spoke I could not refrain from turning to study his face, and the taut lines of his limbs. The strain in his voice seemed all too genuine. Either he was innocent, or he was born to tread the boards. "I have no way of being certain. Has there been any other woman of your household who has gone missing?"

"I...I don't know. I was abroad. If she sent word of the baby, I did not receive it." He looked stunned, appalled even, as if he had been attacked with a sword by a man wild with pride and rage.

The Duke of Rutherford was preparing to kill my cousin; I was certain of it. Eve was stretched out on the ground, cowering in fear, the duke about to deliver the fatal blow. 'Twas unsporting of him; however, his second was doing nothing to prevent him. I threw the man a look of disdain as I launched myself into the fray and took the duke by the shoulder.

I dragged him away from Eve through sheer will; the folly of youth. The duke's anger was only heightened by my actions. I had thought he would calm. Instead, I became the very fuel that drove him. I shall never forget his eyes; large, round, white, and shot through with red. He was not sane, not in the least. His face was purple and as he screamed at me, the veins popped forth from his neck. He knocked me down to the ground with a blood-curdling cry of victory.

Now 'twas I on the ground, cowering in fear. Only, this time, the duke's sword came down. I had the presence of mind to turn my head so that the blow split my lip at the corner of my mouth, slicing a curved line into it. All of that was made known to me later. In that moment, however, I became immediately senseless. I knew only that it was Eve who had rescued me. When I came to, his face was hovering over mine. I wish I had known then what I know now; the man's life was not worth the trauma that followed. The nightmares when I slept, the torment when I was awake, the physical and emotional pain...would I ever be free of it?

Quickly I rose before I was undone by grief. Whether it was due to my pain or the doctor's, I could not say.

Chapter Twelve

The ride home felt twice as long as usual. I was astounded by the emotions that assailed me at what was someone else's tragedy. Whether Dr. Nuttall's grief was newly brought on by the certainty of his wife's death, or provoked by regret for actions taken years before, it mattered not. His suffering felt as if my own, and it took the duration of the journey home to collect myself.

When the groom drew to a halt in the carriage drive of Silvester House, I was surprised to see that the front door stood open. 'Twas not Hatch who stood there in wait of me, but Mrs. Smurthwaite. I had never known less desire to speak with her, but her presence goaded me into taking command of my emotions. I instructed Hatch to send up a tray of tea and biscuits and trudged up the stairs to the green salon, Mrs. S. at my heels.

She strolled into the room as if she were its rightful mistress and seated herself on the divan under the window. When I did not immediately join her, she plumped up the cushions and patted the space at her side.

It was then I realized that I owed her an apology. "I beg your pardon. I failed to call on you the other day as promised."

"I am persuaded there have been more importinet demands on your time."

I could not decide if she were sincere or merely toying with me. "As matters stood, it was rather important. Not more so than honoring my promise to you, however," I said, seating myself by her side. It seemed the least I could do.

She smiled her appreciation. "Did your business have to do with the death of Mrs. Andersen? It was that we were meant to discuss, anyhow."

"It might be connected, yes," I began, but paused when the door opened, and the tea tray was brought in. Mrs. S. poured. She had no need to ask how I took my tea; she was either clairvoyant or she had watched whilst I made it more often than I had ever realized. My hand shook as I took it from her, the cup clattering in its saucer.

"Here," she said, holding out a second plate piled with biscuits and squares of cake. "I daresay you have gone out again without your breakfast. You shall catch your death of one scourgilence or another, should you keep that up."

I laughed at the absurdity of her statement but took the plate and even managed to eat a little.

"Perhaps you had better tell me about it."

I looked down into my cup. "'Tis a terrible story. Are you certain you want to hear it?"

She sat up straight (she was an unrepentant lounger)

and lifted her chin. "But of course! Have you not promised to allow me to help sort through it all?"

"Very well. I cannot say one way or another whether Mrs. Andersen was murdered. She had been ill for some time. It most certainly could have been a natural death. However, her doctor is not who he seems. Some years ago, his young wife..." I choked on the words and cleared my throat. "She perished under mysterious circumstances."

"And you suspect Dr. Nuttall to have murdered her?" Her cup drooped perilously from her fingers.

Miserable, I nodded. "And yet, there is no doubt he loved her. None at all." I wondered why that mattered in the least, and then I knew. I loved Jane and hoped to make her life one of beauty. Was I capable of ending that life for something so small as an act of betrayal? It was an unanswerable question for one who had been so betrayed.

"Hmmm." She placed her tea on the table and took another biscuit. "If he has killed both women, what might the reason be? Why would he behave as if he cared about them and then, open says me! —do away with them?"

I sighed. "In the matter of his wife, she was expecting a child. It is possible when he learned of it he became angry, and..."

"Oh! I see! Well," she scoffed, "we know that was not the circumstates with Mrs. Andersen."

"Do we?" It was a new notion; one that deserved further examination.

"She was too old to conceive; would you not say?"

I felt suddenly very tired. "I would not know. There are some women who look much younger than they are—such as you, Mrs. S." I mustered a smile. "There are others who look older than their years. If Mrs. Andersen married at the same age her daughter currently enjoys, she very well could have been not yet forty when she died."

"Forty!" she exclaimed, her eyes wide. "Well, I would have said a full debacle older. But, she was ill, so that ought to account for it. Still, she needn't have been with child to have betrayed him. Might she have entertained other lovers?" she asked, wiping the crumbs from her chin.

"The obvious possibility is her cousin's husband, but I should be astonished if Mrs. Andersen cared for any man save Dr. Nuttall. She seemed to come alive whenever he was about."

"It is all so very sad. If he is innocent!" she added with a lift of her finger. "As for me, I lost my Georgie much too soon. I thought I should never reconstitute! But, as you see, I contrive."

"I regret life has dealt you such a blow, Mrs. S." I suspected my smile was too wan for warmth. "I should enjoy paying you a call sometime soon. However, I fear that today I must cut short our visit. I have business that cannot wait."

She needed no further urging and put her hand on my arm in a gesture of affection I would have rather enjoyed had she not put all her weight upon it as she stood.

I managed to rise under the strain and led her on my arm to the door. Despite her girth, she rose to the tips of her toes and kissed me on the cheek. I supposed it was meant to cheer me. Rather, it filled me with unutterable sadness. I could not at the time say why. I kissed her hand—it seemed gallant—and shut the door behind her. Then I collapsed onto the divan and slept the sleep of the dead.

As I had no pressing engagements, I was not disturbed. I woke hours later, the night already beginning to set in. I stood, stretched my legs, and pulled the bell; the fire was nearly burnt down. Then I went to the hearth for a means to light the candles. That done, I found I still felt positively dismal. I had no appetite for turning up clues as to the death of either of Miss Andersen's parents, or Mrs. Nuttall. What I wanted more than anything was the fish at Stevens in Bond Street.

The notion cheered me and I took myself up to my chamber, calling for Jack as I went. He was as prompt as usual. "There you are!" I teased. "If I had to wait any longer I would find it needful to stretch out on the bed!"

Jack did not so much as smile.

I bit back a further jibe and went to the clothespress. "I am abominably wrinkled. I shall require a new shirt and cravat at the least."

He brushed me aside (I knew I would have to keep him forever; he was ruined for anyone with reasonable expectations of a valet) and collected what was required. I sat on the bed and looked down at the ring on my hand. Why I wore the symbol of an action in which I no longer took pride, I could not say. It was handsome enough, but I feared it did not lend me the consequence I desired. Removing it, I tossed it into my jewel case.

Jack, unlike any valet I had employed since the marring of my mouth, took pride in my appearance. He noted my fingers were now unadorned and chose for me a sapphire ring. Then he dressed me in a blue-spotted waistcoat to match. He tidied up my hair with pomade and lavender water and sent me out into the world looking my best.

By the time the coachman deposited me in front of Stevens, I was feeling much more the thing. I spotted Walter in the foyer as I stood at the open door. He called to me and I was admitted, passing off my coat and cane to the attendant.

"Where have you been, old man? I haven't seen you for what must be a fortnight!"

"It cannot have been that long, can it?" I felt the weight on my heart lift further as I clapped my friend on the back. "'Tis good to see you," I said as we took our seats at a table for two. "What have you been up to?"

"You mean since you dined *en famille* Leavitt?" He rolled his eyes. "Father has not ceased discoursing on the Andersen scandal. What's more, he has learned you are attempting to get to the bottom of it. I have never seen him angrier." He smiled wolfishly, as if he enjoyed my predicament.

"Do not tell me you agree with him!"

He stared at me, goggle-eyed. "Did I not tell you I have

no wish for you to make murder your business? I must think of my sister's reputation."

I felt as if I had been dealt a blow to the face by an unseen assailant. "But you do not believe such things can harm Jane, do you?"

"How could they not?" He leaned forward in his seat. "Give it up, Trev. It shall not serve you, in the end. There are none to thank you for your assistance in the Gilbert tragedy."

I knew well enough the truth of his words. Every person I helped in that particular course of truth-seeking had turned against me. I felt my happy future with Jane start to slip through my fingers. "There is very little to go on," I admitted. "I do not know what I would do next in order to discover the truth. I have spoken to everyone and I seem to know less than I did before."

By the time the food arrived, Walter and I were discussing other matters. However, I was not as hungry as I ought to have been and merely picked at my plate.

"Is the turbot not to your liking?" he asked.

I did not deign to reply.

"Come, old man, you mustn't fret! If it will put you at ease, let us talk about it. I shan't be any help," he said, shoveling the better part of a pigeon pie into his mouth, "but I am willing to listen."

"Very well, then." I was not as eager as I made out to be. "There is currently only one person under suspicion. He is called Dr. Nuttall."

141

"Now that," Walter said, brandishing his fork, "is a strange man."

"On what do you base your opinion?"

"I heard he was betrothed to a young woman before he met the Andersens. He broke it off, just like that! It is said she retired—somewhere or other," he said with a shrug, "under a cloud. Maybe *she* killed Mrs. Andersen," he suggested, laughing as if it were some great joke.

I ignored it, as I did most of Walter's taunting. "Yes, Lady Marlowe mentioned her, as well. However, if this woman he spurned did indeed quit town, how might she have had the opportunity to commit murder? Which brings me to my next point: I do not know for a certainty that Mrs. Andersen was killed. It might well have been death by illness."

"Let's pray that is the case, for everyone involved." He grinned, lifting his brows clownishly as he chewed.

"I suppose it possible someone outside of the household could have put a period to her existence." No longer the least interested in food or conversation, I rose to my feet. "Do be a good boy and find out to where the former betrothed of Dr. Nuttall has escaped."

Walter looked up at me in exasperation. "Which lady?"

"The one he cast aside." I was beginning to like the physician less and less.

"Oh, very well, if you insist," he chided, returning his gaze to his plate.

"Thank you, Walter," I said with deep sincerity. "It means a great deal more than you know."

"If you say so, Trev." He waved his fingers at me dismissively as he tucked into his second plate of food.

I sent the coachman on his way and walked home. I had drunk far more than I had eaten and was a trifle woozy. Making a mental note to refrain from such unwise habits in future I strolled along, unmolested. I had no fear despite the dark alleys between homes. After several scares whilst investigating Johnny Gilbert's death, I had invested in a walking stick that concealed a wicked blade.

It was small, stealthy and, most important, invisible, a comforting feature since having been sliced in the face by a sword. The knowledge that it was there gave me a sense of security I greatly valued. Nevertheless, I did not expect the attack that came shortly before I turned the corner onto Grosvenor Square. It was one ruffian only—nothing I could not handle—but by the time I had drawn my sword he was gone.

Once I had recovered from the shock of colliding with a large person who came towards me at a dead run, I realized it was more a matter of theft than violence to my person. I put my hands into all of my pockets. Nothing was missing. However, I was surprised to find a piece of folded parchment. I drew it out and held it under the light of a nearby street lamp. Squinting, I tried to make out the words and realized it had been written backwards. After some deliberation, I deciphered its meaning:

Stay away from Marlowe House. You shall not learn the truth. You can't help. There is nothing to be done.

I read it again and considered. Who knew I was investigating Dr. Nuttall other than him? Only Walter, Mrs. S., Jack, Miss Andersen, and perhaps Sir Thomas and Lady Marlowe. There were servants in the household of whom I had asked questions, as well: the butler, the housekeeper, and a maid. She was a pretty girl who had clearly formed a *tendre* for the doctor, and whom she had confessed to encountering often. Perhaps it was she who wished to protect him as well.

I slid the paper into my waistcoat pocket and resumed my journey, lost in thought. So far Dr. Nuttall had a dead wife, a fiancée he had spurned, a woman with whom he had an indeterminate relationship, and now quite possibly a devotee amongst the servants. He was handsome and intelligent, but so was I. Why were women so charmed by him? And often to their destruction, if my suspicions were correct.

After my long nap, I was not in the least sleepy. My emotions, however, had fatigued me in other ways. I sat on my own by the fire in the green salon, deep into the night. A distant voice in my mind insisted there was some party I was meant to attend, but I ignored it. A row of elegant invitations lined the mantel, but I refused to consult them, as I wished to be alone. I knew if I went to my bed Willy would appear, but for some reason neither did I wish to speak with him.

It was early the next morning when I dragged myself to my room and threw myself onto the bed fully clothed. When I awoke Willy waited, just as I knew he would.

"You look dreadful! I think perhaps you had too much to drink last night."

I lifted my head from my pillow to give him the full effect of my scathing glare and allowed it to drop again.

"Am I to believe you had *nothing* to drink last night?"

With a groan I rolled onto my back, my eyes screwed shut against the light streaming through the window. "I would have you know there is something between too much and nothing."

"How has a 'something' to drink last night resulted in such suffering this morning?"

I cracked open a lid to find him hovering over me. "How do you do that? I never hear a sound unless you speak. One second you are here and the next you are gone."

He pulled a face. "Have you discovered anything new as to Mrs. Andersen's mysterious death?"

I pushed myself up to sit against the pillows. "Her personal physician is a likely candidate for murder. Or perhaps it was an accident. It is no simple thing to prescribe such dangerous medicines." I might have told him of the bones I had witnessed, including the tiny skull, but had no desire to speak of them again to anyone.

"And what of the daughter? How does she fare?"

I had just been wondering the same. "I think I had best call on her today. I have not seen her since before..." I looked up to see Willy staring at me in consternation, a frown on his face. "What?" I demanded.

"Nothing," he insisted. "Only, I think you must have

145

had a rough time of it these past few days. You look tired, but it's more than that. Have you hurt yourself somehow?"

My hand flew to the lump on my head. "Yes, but I am well enough; nearly mended. It shall not impede me in my course."

"And what might that be, Trev?"

"To call on Miss Andersen." I hopped out of bed. "I have many more questions to ask."

Chapter Thirteen

I decided it best to again bring Jane with me to Marlowe House. It would require that I put off my visit until late morning or early afternoon when such visits were expected. I went to my desk and scratched out a note to be taken to Leavitt House requesting her company. "Jack!" I called, but he did not immediately appear.

A glance around the room indicated that he had been in—the fire had been attended to and the curtains opened. Had he allowed a maid to do it, I would have wakened sooner. "Jack!" I called again, but still nothing. Striding to the door, I jerked it open and was confronted with the terrified gaze of a girl. I could not think what could be the source of her fear until, finally, I realized the light streaming through the window behind me had rendered my nightshirt nearly useless as a garment intended to obscure my nakedness.

"Damnation!" I shouted and slammed the door in her face. I could hear her soft cries as she ran along the passage to the door that led to the servant staircase. In her zeal to escape, she let it bang shut behind her. "Jack!" I bellowed, far louder than I had intended.

Finally he appeared with head hung low, a curtain of hair obscuring his face.

"What is this?" I demanded. "It is not like you to be tardy. And your hair is a disgrace."

He shook his head which still hung low, as if he were guilty of some crime.

Placing my finger under his chin, I lifted his face out from under the fall of hair. I was forced to bite my tongue so as not to gasp aloud. One of his eyes was purple and black and it was evident his nose would never be entirely straight again.

He turned his gaze from mine as if he could not bear the scrutiny.

"What have you done?" I asked sharply.

"Nuttin'," he insisted.

"Do tell me your opponent had the worst of it!" I demanded, assuming he had enjoyed his first brawl.

He jerked his chin free and turned to the clothespress to select the day's attire.

"Do you not own a mirror, boy?" Taking him from behind by the shoulders, I propelled him over to mine. "See there? 'Tis a face that has met with a fist."

He scowled. "'Tis nuttin'," he repeated, strangely subdued.

"Had it to do with a young lady?" Over the top of his head I caught the reflection of my foolish grin.

He hid his expression behind his hair again. "No." His voice came very low.

I began to feel more alarmed than annoyed. "You have done nothing to alert the constable, have you?"

He shook his head.

"Jack," I said, turning him to face me. "You must tell me what has happened."

Rather than flinch he stared back at me, defiant.

I began to understand. "Does it have to do with me?" I asked in disbelief. His gaze dropped from mine and I repeated my question, this time with a little shake of his shoulders.

His scowl was fierce. "Alrigh' then! I'm to tell ya to stop askin' questions at Marlowe 'ouse."

"Then it is on account of me!" I cried, as angry as I was apprehensive.

He did not reply, but the look of terror on his face prompted me to turn abruptly away to collect myself. "Did you recognize the fellow who did this to you?"

"No."

I turned to him again. "You must try to remember. Might it have been a servant from Marlowe House?"

"Dunno," he said. "I ne'er seen 'im afore."

"Was he tall? Short? Did he dress well or have an accent?" I urged.

"I dunno. I din' see 'im. I jus' 'eard wha' I tol' ya."

"Very well," I said, though I wished to ask more questions. To further shame him with unanswerable queries,

149

however, was intolerable. I nodded, and he resumed his duties in silence. As we went about the business of dressing, I began to relax. I realized it would be folly to bring Jane to Marlowe House after the warning Jack received. And yet I longed to see her. I had not been to Leavitt House since my return to town. I decided to take her for a carriage ride to the park. I would arrive unannounced, as I had yet to have the note delivered, but I trusted she would still be glad to see me. "I shall require my whip," I said quietly.

Jack collected it and put it into my hand. It was my intention to quit the room without another word but I thought better of it. Instead I paused on the pretext of examining my coiffure in the mirror. "Relay these instructions to Cook: she is to give you a cold mutton chop to put on that eye every day until it is less unsightly."

"Yes, Your Lordship," he said.

"A fresh chop each day or it shall not serve!" I warned, fingering my curls despite their perfection.

"Yes, my lord."

"And when you are done with it for the day, tell her to cook it up for you. Heaven forbid she should mistakenly serve it to me for my supper."

He nodded, somewhat nonplussed.

"It shall not be worth eating should it not be paired with fried onions." I clandestinely watched his reflection in the glass whilst tweaking a fold in my cravat. "And croquette potatoes." I knew they were a favorite of his. "And some Plum Flummery would not go amiss." His eyes grew wide and I bit back a smile. "I shall expect to have some myself, so take care not to eat it all."

"Yes, sir!"

I stepped across the threshold, shut the door, and was nearly to the landing before he let out a crow of delight. Laughing, I raced down the staircase and the next to the front hall, the capes of my greatcoat flaring to life behind me. Hatch had anticipated my wish to take out the curricle, so I had no need to wait. He threw open the door and I strode through and directly into the equipage, its top up to deflect any rain that might fall on my journey.

Whistling all the way, I arrived sooner than I had anticipated. As I pulled on the reins, I glanced up at the window of the salon on the first floor. I knew well enough what to expect. By the time my carriage had ground to a halt, the lady of the house would have spied me through the window and decided whether she would be home to me. This morning, however, despite the earliness of the hour, I was confident Jane would be delighted to receive me.

I did not wait for the butler who answered the door to present my card. Rather, I took myself up the stairs, brushed past the footman who guarded the salon door, and opened it myself to find Jane standing in the middle of the room, her eyes twinkling.

"Julian!" she cried as she ran to me.

I opened my arms and we enjoyed a brief embrace before her mother made her presence known. It did naught to quell my happiness. "Good morning!" I said in greeting to both ladies. "Jane, go put on your hat and we shall ride through the park."

"Splendid!" She gave me a coy look out from under her mother's watchful eye as she passed.

I turned to watch her go, my heart pounding. It had been some time since we had enjoyed any privacy, and it was my intention to make use of our ride to steal a kiss.

"I see you still intend to marry my daughter," Mrs. Leavitt said.

I whirled about in surprise. "Why should I not?" I had not yet realized the import of her words.

She pressed her folded hands tight against her stomach. "The Andersens; it is said that you cannot leave well enough alone."

I frowned. "You have had this from your son?"

"And others. My husband is angry, indeed."

Doubtless not as angry as I was with Walter. "I find I cannot think why it is a concern of yours, or anyone else's for that matter."

She sighed. "My husband's objections are plain enough. As for myself, I wonder how it appears to others that you are promised to my daughter but pass the time with another?"

I laughed, relieved. "If that is what troubles you, you need not fear. Jane has accompanied me to Marlowe House. She is fully aware of why I go there; she approves of it, in fact."

Mrs. Leavitt's expression hardened. "I rather doubt it. I have done my best to keep the rumors from her, but I can do nothing about the rest of Society. I will not have my daughter made fodder for the scandal sheets."

I laughed again, this time in disbelief. "I had not thought you a woman who would be troubled by something so illusory. I would have married your daughter a year ago if it had been allowed!"

"And until you do marry her, you shall take care to protect her good name."

Troubled, I put a hand to my chin and stroked the scar at the corner of my mouth. "I assure you, there is nothing in my visits to Marlowe House about which to be concerned."

She shrugged. "What you do is none of my affair. How my daughter is perceived in Society is, however. You must refrain from calling on Miss Andersen so openly."

"Who has said that I call on Miss Andersen? I have been but twice!"

She produced a piece of parchment from her pocket and held it out to me.

I recognized the size and the manner in which it was folded. It was also written backwards as had been the one I received the night previous. It read: *All the world laughs at your daughter. What will they think if he can't stay away from Miss Andersen long enough to wed?*

The handwriting was simple and plain, much the same as the other. There was something else about it that niggled at me, but I could not immediately identify what it might be. "Thank you for allowing me to read this, Mrs. Leavitt. May I keep it?"

She looked surprised. "Why, yes, I suppose so. What can it hurt?"

"Thank you." I sketched a bow and took myself off to the front hall to wait for Jane. She arrived in short order and I led her out to the carriage on my arm. It was a day of sunshine and possibilities, but I found my previous cheer had wilted.

"What is it?" she asked once we had driven off. "Are we to call on Miss Andersen?"

I smiled and was gratified when her eyes softened. Sadly, my next words were sure to trouble her. "Your mother has taken exception to my meddling in their affairs."

She sighed. "There is nothing in that to surprise anyone."

"Indeed, but 'tis for a reason I cannot tolerate."

"You, my love, are intolerant of much," she said, laughing. "What is one more?"

Indignant, I gave her a mock glare. "Intolerant! I would hardly describe myself as such. 'Tis for a reason that shall make you apprehensive as well."

"Oh! Well then," she said thoughtfully, "you had better tell me."

"Very well. You were correct in suspecting some would believe I dance attendance on Miss Andersen. Whether they think me to be courting her or ruining her, it does not matter; the rumors are disconcerting. Your reputation shall suffer as a result."

"I did warn you about that, it is true," she said slowly,

"but who is there to know you have called on Miss Andersen? And do they say I was with you nearly every time you have met?" Before I could reply she plunged on. "I believe someone is trying to cause you difficulty, to distract and defeat you. Someone wants you to stop calling at Marlowe House—so you do not find the killer."

At the time, I did not give enough weight to her words; I know that now. "If there is, indeed, a killer. She might well have died of natural causes or been accidentally overdosed."

"Have the authorities asked the proper questions? There must have been a physician who can say how it was she died."

"I do believe that would be Dr. Nuttall. I shall ask him questions about that as well, though it shall be no assurance if it were he who killed her."

"Yes, I believe you must. Now, let speak of other things," she said, her voice soft and low. "It has been too long since we have been alone together." She linked both her arms with mine and leaned her head on my shoulder.

I could not restrain a smile, though she did not benefit from it. The moment we came to a section of the road free of prying eyes, I drew the horses to a halt and removed my hat. Using it to shield our faces, I ducked under the brim of her bonnet and put my lips to hers. They were warm and softer than I had recalled. I groaned from the sweetness of her mouth against mine and the deepening of my need for more.

It would not do, however, for anyone to speak ill of the

woman about to become my wife. With a sigh, I lifted my head and replaced my hat. Taking her hand, I pressed a fervent kiss upon it. With a look that was meant to convey everything I dared not say, I whipped the horses and resumed our journey to the park.

She clung again to my arm with both of hers and was so quiet I wondered if perhaps she had fallen asleep. I was content to let her be for the present. I was humbled and delighted she had not become hysterical over the rumors about me and Miss Andersen. I contemplated the many reasons to be proud of my future wife. If only her father would allow us to set a specific date! If he did not do so before the end of winter, I decided that I would simply obtain a special license and take her to wife in the front hall of Silvester House.

My carefree attitude returned, and it was with renewed vigor that I drove my team to the park. We had just turned in at the barrier, when a carriage pulled up alongside us. A woman in an elegant hat rolled down the glass and called out to me.

"Lady Jersey," I called back in surprise. "You are out and about early this morning!"

"My lord," she cried, her expression harried. "I have just heard the most dreadful news!"

"My condolences. I shall yield the road so that you might pass," I began.

"You do not understand! It is not I who has suffered a tragedy. It is Miss Andersen. Her cousin has met with a horrid accident. I am afraid she is dead!"

I turned to Jane in disbelief; she looked to share my horror. When I returned my attention to Lady Jersey, her carriage had already moved on.

"Poor Miss Andersen!" Jane exclaimed. "I cannot imagine what it is she must feel."

"Lady Jersey said it was an accident," I mused, a notion forming in my mind.

"If Mrs. Andersen was overdosed, also by accident, that would be two such tragedies in as many weeks," Jane observed.

"It does rather beg belief, does it not?"

"Why? What can you mean?"

"Perhaps Lady Marlowe saw something that would identify Mrs. Andersen's killer."

"But, did you not say her death was an accident?"

I considered the letters and the violent warning via Jack. "Another accident? It hardly seems likely. What if he *had* accidentally overdosed her? I doubt he would commit murder to cover it up. If he did take Mrs. Andersen's life by intention, however, there is no limit to what a man like that might do." I had encountered at least one such person in my lifetime. There were doubtless other such fiends capable of doing away with as many people required to achieve the desired result.

"But would his reputation as a physician not be ruined if anyone were to learn he had caused her death, even by accident? Might that not be a motive for murder?"

"Yes, your argument does have merit. I can hardly call

on any of the residents of Marlowe House today, however. We might as well continue with our ride."

Jane agreed and so we enjoyed ourselves for a time, but she could sense my heart was no longer in it. I could think of nothing but those letters and who might have written them. It seemed wise to obtain a sample of Dr. Nuttall's handwriting. For, truthfully, this was not the second accidental death in the physician's past; there was his wife for whom to account. I felt my heart harden—I knew I must not stop until this man was no longer at liberty to kill another.

Chapter Fourteen

I delayed until after Lady Marlowe's funeral before I returned to her home. I was determined to discover what I could from Dr. Nuttall. I had learned that she had fallen down the stairs; as usual, Society were rife with rumors. However, whether it was an accident or intentional seemed very possibly unknowable. If Dr. Nuttall had pushed Lady Marlowe to her death, I feared the truth might never come to light.

I chose to be driven in the closed carriage to Marlowe House as the weather had again turned quite cold. As the horses persevered through a driving rain, I changed my mind and decided the best course of action would be to first question Miss Andersen. I had not counted on Sir Thomas, however. He entered the salon with his cousin-in-law and took a greater interest in her welfare than he had any other time we had met. I thought it odd and wondered if something unseemly might be happening between them.

Upon their arrival, I rose, and we greeted one another. Miss Andersen chose to sit in the center of the divan. Sir

Thomas took up his seat far closer to her than I was allowed to sit next to my betrothed. I sat in a chair directly across, which afforded me an illuminating view of their silent communication.

"I had hoped to see you, Miss Andersen, to express my condolences. As you are here as well, Sir Thomas, please know how sorry I am for the loss of your wife. What a dreadful time it has been for the both of you."

"Indeed, yes," he said, his eyes reddening.

"I had also hoped to ask Miss Andersen some questions pertaining to the death of her mother." I looked to her for a response, but none was forthcoming.

"She is very cut up about it," Sir Thomas said. She buried her face in her handkerchief and he put his arm around her shoulders. "Now, now, my dear, it shall be all right."

I frowned, troubled by my suspicions as to the nature of their relationship. "Is Dr. Nuttall still in residence?"

"It is he who has determined that my dear wife fell down the stairs. She caught her heel on the hem of her gown and down she went. 'Tis a sad loss. A sad loss, indeed."

I could not help but doubt his explanation. My observations had taught me that the current fashions allowed a delicious peek of the ankles. I looked again to Miss Andersen to read her reaction, but she still wept softly into the lacy white folds of muslin. "How dreadful!" I dutifully responded. "And unexpected. I must thank you for seeing me at such a difficult time."

"Not at all. No, indeed, we would not dream of denying you entrance, would we, Hannah?"

She shook her head but did not look up.

"Miss Andersen, I am sorry for your grief. I had not known you were so fond of Lady Marlowe."

This produced a reaction. Gently, she wiped her eyes and sighed. "I was, of course," she said with a glance at Sir Thomas. "I am also distressed and very much afraid for..."

Light began to dawn. "For Dr. Nuttall? Why is that?" I gently prodded.

"I don't know exactly. Only, he was the physician who attended at the death of both my mother and Lady Marlowe, and I fear someone shall wonder at the oddness of it. Two deaths in so short a time...might not someone become suspicious?"

I was impressed by her insight and wondered what might account for it. Was she in love with the doctor? Was Sir Thomas in love with *her*? Could he have pushed his wife down the stairs so as to wed Miss Andersen? Matters appeared to be more complicated than I had suspected. "Have the authorities been asking such questions?"

"'Tis nothing with which we cannot cope," Sir Thomas said. "I am not a man entirely without influence. Should anyone hurt Hannah, they shall have to answer to me."

"How would implicating Dr. Nuttall hurt Miss Andersen?" I thought better of the question too late. I very much wished to know the answer, but I was certain I would not receive one that resembled the truth.

161

Indeed, Miss Andersen blushed to the roots of her hair, and Sir Thomas coughed into his fist at such length I was forced to believe I was not wanted. It seemed clear Miss Andersen had a *tendre* for the physician. Why did he not simply tell her mother the truth? Would Mrs. Andersen not give her consent to the physician to wed her daughter? Or was it simply easier to do away with her and avoid the possible turmoil it induced?

I was reminded of Lady Marlowe's patent distress when Jane and I had come to offer Miss Andersen our condolences. Did she see something that put her in danger? I took my leave not one whit wiser than I had been when I arrived.

Evening had fallen by the time I returned home. There were no plans to escort Jane anywhere, for which I was grateful; the weather was filthy, and I had no wish to go out again. I instructed Hatch to send my dinner up to my chamber on a tray. Ridding myself of my shoes without Jack's help was simple; the coat, however, was another matter. I contrived but would find it needful to request he have the ripped seams repaired. By the time I had donned my dressing gown, the tray had arrived. Suddenly fearful that Willy, with whom I had no wish to converse, would appear, I took up the tray and descended to the music room in my slippers.

I ate my meal in front of the fire with only my thoughts for company. Allowing my gaze to roam, I realized I was in possession of a great number of objects I had been taking for granted. Chief amongst them was the pianoforte in the corner of the room. It had been long since I had played.

My desire to rectify my neglect grew with each bite until the urge to play became irresistible. Cleaning my hands on a napkin, I went to the instrument and took up a seat on the bench adorned with my mother's needlepoint creation. It was placed at an angle under a window which afforded a view of the square, as well as a comfortable proximity to the fire. When my fingers touched the keys, I was overcome by the kinship I felt. Had they not been untouched, unloved, and banished to the corner of a room rarely frequented? Rather than succumb to despair over the past, my heart flooded with gratitude for Jane and her acceptance of my shortcomings.

I had played through several variations of Mozart's 'Ah! vous dirai-je Maman,' when I noticed that a closed carriage had drawn to a halt outside the house next to mine. Idly, I wondered who had come to call on Mrs. S. Grateful she would be occupied rather than at my side in expectation of being entertained, I gave the matter no further thought. However, when the door to the music room opened to admit Hatch bearing a card on a silver tray, I was somewhat taken aback. When I read the name on the card, I was thoroughly astonished.

I returned the card to Hatch with a look of scorn. "It seems I have neglected a portion of your education," I said, starting on another variation. "I needs must rectify that. It shall doubtless be at great cost to your comfort."

"Very good, my lord," he said with a deep bow. It was therefore a reason for further astonishment when he returned moments later with my cousin at his elbow.

I slammed my hands down upon the keyboard and leapt to my feet. "Hatch, my instructions were to deny Mr. Rogers-Reimann entrance without exception!"

"Don't be ridiculous, Trev," Eve replied. "He has known me since I was a child. I *am* a member of the family, after all."

Hatch turned on his heel and quit the room whilst I attempted to withhold my wrath. "You are here now," I observed. "May I ask why?"

"Why else?" Eve riposted, his shaggy brows waggling.

"Indulge me."

"Very well, then," he said as he slunk across the room towards me, picking up and discarding various ornaments as he came.

Apprehension flared, caught as I was between the piano and the hearth with the window at my back. I felt cornered, like a fox in its hole, surrounded by baying dogs and a bugler announcing all within its scope of my imminent demise. "I am waiting." My voice was strong and sure, as if it belonged to someone else entirely.

"Indeed, you have waited quite some time for this particular pronouncement."

I knew, then, what he wanted. The boon. "What shall it be? One of my maids to ravish? Or does your depravity require something more sordid. The boot boy, perhaps?" I despised myself for saying it the moment it was out.

Eve's mouth twisted into a gruesome smile. "I shall accept your bet and raise you two boot boys." And still he came towards me, his step heavy and measured.

I burned with fury. "Very well, then; a ride to hell in my carriage it is."

He paused in his advance and vented an overblown sigh. "Really, Trev. I had thought you sufficiently humbled by now. But, have no fear; you shall grovel properly when I have done with you."

I looked into his eyes and saw nothing but venom. I wondered what could have caused such animosity in him. I had done nothing to deserve it. "I shall insist that you remember your promise—that you would not ask of me anything that goes against my scruples."

"Ah!" he said with a lift of his finger. "That is true. No, the boon I am about to request— nay, insist upon—shall tally very well with your conscience, my dear."

I felt myself relax; I was fool enough to trust him, this one last time. "What is it, then?"

"Merely that you cry off from your betrothal to Miss Leavitt, that I might marry her instead." His smile was unremarkable but paired with such words he looked the very devil.

There was little point in becoming angry over such a request; it was too ridiculous. "Why should I? Even if I were to do so, she would never have you."

"Oh, I think she might."

"No. She would not. Of this I am quite certain. Either

165

way, 'tis a moot point," I said through gritted teeth, "as I shall not do as you ask."

"Shan't you? Have you forgotten the depths of depravity to which I am willing to plumb? What of Miss Ashley, the maiden whose rescue you rushed to, only to learn that she had been in my arms the night previous?"

"You lied as to your plans," I ground out.

He grinned at me, his face distorted far more than mine when offering my fiercest frown. "And I shall lie again. And again, and again. As often as is needful until I have what I want."

I began to know fear. It squeezed my lungs and banged against my ribs. "And what might that be? To see me destroyed? Or is it Jane you want in particular? Perhaps this is about her dowry," I said, disgusted. "Haven't you enough money?"

"'Tis all of those things," he said with a spread of his fleshy white hands. "She is rich, she is beautiful, and she is yours. It's so simple, it's child's play. I have so much to gain and you so much to lose," he soothed, as if his words were a comfort.

This was it. This was the test. Would I allow myself to give in to fear, or would I stand tall in defense of what I knew was right? "I shall not do it! There is nothing you can say to change that. I refuse, utterly." I felt supremely righteous, and only slightly less confident. The subject upon which I was yet deluded was the magnitude of Evelyn Roger-Reimann's immeasurable wickedness.

"I believe you shall," he said, as if it were a walk in the rain under discussion. "If you do not agree, I shall set in motion the most appalling scandal."

"I am well-acquainted with scandal," I began, but he cut me off.

"Do you think I mean to spread gossip about *you?* No, no, no, my dear! That has been done, and quite effectively, if I am allowed to say so. No—I mean to spread rumors about Miss Leavitt!"

I felt the blood drain from my face even before I had begun to consider the sort of rumors to which he referred. "Whatever you say of her, no one shall believe it," I hotly insisted, though I knew such a statement was akin to tilting at windmills.

"I think they shall. Gossip, you see, is rather like music." He ran his fingers along the keys of the pianoforte. "It fills the room, every nook and cranny. It finds its way between the walls and whistles along the rafters until the entire house is filled with it."

The fear I had been holding at bay rose up like a wave about to crash onto the shore. "You are angry with me, Eve— with *me!* Do not do this to an innocent young woman. You are livid that I meant to rescue Miss Ashley from your wretched advances; angrier still that I saved her from the exile to which she was reduced, and by her own father! She is far beyond your reach now, and it eats at you."

He threw back his head and laughed. "I am not troubled by the state of my soul, Trev. I cannot fathom why it should trouble you."

He was almost upon me where I stood by the window. I wondered if he would push me out of it and whether I would prefer that to the fate to which he hoped to consign me.

"It will be the simplest of tasks," he insisted. "I have boasted *ad nauseum* as to my exploits with Miss Ashley. 'Twas so successful her father, as you say, disowned her entirely. I need only suggest Miss Leavitt is of the same caliber."

"It will not matter. I shall marry her anyway!"

"I do believe you would, Trev, truly I do." He studied me with a mild interest. "But I suspect you are not seeing the situation from Miss Leavitt's point of view. Do you believe she would willingly saddle you with her scandal if she might do otherwise?"

"Well, I..." The question had struck me dumb.

"I think not," he murmured, again moving towards me. "And when she chooses not to marry you, I shall be there to pick up the pieces. As you know, I am not in the least particular when it comes to my reputation. It shall be the *ondit* of town for a fortnight or so, but I have survived worse."

"Have you, Eve? Was it not I who endured the scandal of your duel with Rutherford? All this time you have allowed Society to believe it was I who deserved his wrath!"

"Allowed, my dear? That is not the word I would employ." He stood mere inches from me now. The heaving of my embittered breast nearly pressed against the jeweled stickpin in his cravat. "Rather, I urged them to believe it.

Indeed, I would go so far as to say 'twas I who conceived of the notion from the start."

There was no point in commenting on this fresh betrayal. My only thought was for Jane. "I shall not allow you to do this, Eve!"

"How are you to prevent it? If you do not spurn her, I shall tell everyone she knows I have had her already. If you do, I shall comfort her in her sorrow. No one else shall want her once she has been jilted. Either way, she becomes my wife. The only choice you have to make is how she is to be wounded. Shall it be the pain of your rejection, or that of all Society including her mushroom of a father?"

I stood before my looking glass and scrutinized the scar that proclaimed my shame to all, and for the rest of time. Would it prevent Miss Jane Leavitt from accepting my offer of marriage? When I was with her, I forgot about the cut that marked me. I smiled without thinking; I laughed brightly. She thought me handsome and said as much. Nor did she blame me for the choices I had made that put me beneath the duke's sword. To her credit, the fact I had discovered Johnny Gilbert's killer led her to admire me. More to the point, her acceptance of my flaws restored me to Society's good graces. It was the world in which I belonged.

Perhaps some say that I might do better than Miss Jane Leavitt, but I could not think how. Without her I would be nothing. I looked into the reflection of my eyes and knew she would consent to stand by my side as my wife. With a wink for the man in the glass, I was off to seal my fate.

A growl rose in my throat, its strength only matched by

the power in my arms as I put my hands to his chest and shoved him with all my might.

His eyes widened in surprise, but he did not cry out until he staggered under my weight and caught his foot on the stones of the hearth. He fell quickly to the floor, throwing out both hands to break his fall, one of which landed in the hot coals. With an almighty roar, he dragged his burnt hand to his chest and wailed his pain.

I pulled the bell and stood over my cousin in wait of assistance. I had never seen anyone so pitiful or so unworthy of my compassion.

"You shall pay for this night's work!" he roared. "I swear that you shall!"

It was all I could do to refrain from landing a knee to his chest and putting my hands around his throat. "Have I not paid enough for your villainy?" I shouted. "You have come here to threaten and insult me and my intended bride, and still 'tis me you blame? I shall tell you once and only once—you shall never have Jane! She is far braver than you know."

"We shall see about that!" he bawled. "You have only until spring to inform me of your acquiescence!"

Hatch knocked and, upon entering the room, recoiled in horror. "What are we to do, my lord?"

"Have someone pick him up off of my floor and deposited into his carriage. What becomes of him after that, I care not."

Upon Hatch's departure, Eve became hysterical. "You

shall regret this treatment! I am wounded! Can you not see? What kind of man abandons his wounded relative? What if I had abandoned you when it was Rutherford who wished for your blood? Or after you were injured? Did I not bring you home to my own bed and have you tended there until you had recovered?"

I stared at him, my chest heaving with indignation, leaving me no air for idle speech.

Hatch returned with two footmen, who looked a question at me.

"Take him out to his carriage and see to it he is driven away. I will not have him in my house another moment."

They scurried to do as I asked. Eve's screams intensified the farther away from me he was taken. When I heard them rise from the pavement below, I turned to the cool panes of the window and studied the top of his carriage. His cries of rage were still audible even after the door had closed against them. I did not move until the conveyance pulled away, but that was not the end of his cries. I heard them still as I lay in bed and attempted to sleep. Willy sat in his chair but did not speak to me, or I to him.

Chapter Fifteen

Time passed, but not my determination to thwart my cousin. More to the point, the day was fast approaching for me to insist that Jane's father allow us to set a specific date for the wedding. Willy, however, had much to say on the matter.

"You cannot possibly mean to wed her in light of Roger-Reimann's threats!"

"I am not afraid of him," I insisted, drawing back the blankets from the bed in preparation to retire.

"You ought to be. If it were not for Jane, you might still be taking your supper in the music room every night."

I paused from splashing my face at the washbasin to throw him a sharp look. "How do you know where I dine?"

"How could I not? You treated us to those tedious Mozart variations once too often at school."

I grunted my acknowledgement. "Did you know 'twas he who put about the rumor that it was I who dallied with Rutherford's wife? And all this time I thought the duke to blame."

"It was most likely both who created that scandal, Trev. What difference can it make?"

"I had believed him to be my friend in those days. I had thought it was I who was done with him, not he who was determined to ruin me."

"And do you know his nature better now than you did before this most recent encounter?"

Sighing, I toweled my face dry. "No, I suppose not."

There was a pause before Willy asked, "What do you intend to do about Miss Leavitt?"

"I do not know. I insisted there was nothing he could do or say that would stop me from marrying her. But what if he is right about whether she shall marry me once he carries out his threats? What you said is true; if it were not for her, I might still be unwelcome everywhere. How might I give her up? What shall I do without her?"

He shook his head, his smile melancholy.

"It could be true, that she will refuse to marry me once he has lied about her." I sat on the bed, my fists clenched. "I cannot begin to imagine the pain she shall feel if she believes I might be dragged down again because of her. But it shall not be because of her!" I pounded my fists into the mattress. "It shall be because of him!"

"It shan't change the truth, Trev. She is too aware of how much your reputation has already endured. She would marry nearly anyone else before she marries you."

"Even Eve?" I snarled.

"He is not the worst I have known."

"I wish I could say the same. If he were insane I might find a way to excuse him, even forgive him, but he is not. He is quite simply malevolent."

"You have not answered my question," he said quietly.

I stood and paced the room, the heat of the fire warming my bare legs with each pass. "There is only one thing I may do."

"You cannot intend to tell her the truth! She would rather die than put you through such a choice."

"That is what I fear most; that she shall irrevocably remove herself from the situation. So, I shall devise a test, some hypothetical circumstance that mirrors the reality. I shall lay it out before her and ask her what she would do. Then I shall know."

When I looked to the chair in the window, Willy was gone. It was just as well; I was spent. Blowing out the candle, I climbed into bed. A sliver of moonlight played along the wall on the far side of the room. It was but a streak of light, but I found that if I concentrated on it my thoughts stilled enough to fall asleep.

When I awoke I suddenly knew what must be done. After breakfast I went to my desk and drew forth three sheets of parchment. On one I wrote a letter to Jane informing her that the wedding was off. I could not, at the time, perceive how cold and terse it was but, in truth, I took no trouble over it. I truly thought it would never be delivered. Despite my anxieties, I believed Jane could weather any storm that came her way. On the second sheet I wrote her a warning of what was to come and begged her to stand by me, no matter what. On the third, I worked out the scenario I would put to her the next time I saw her. Only then would I know with certainty which of the missives I would have delivered.

Feeling as if a burden were lifted, I picked up the morning's correspondence. It proved to be the usual mix of duns and invitations. However, there was a letter addressed in a hand I did not immediately recognize. I broke open the seal and unfolded the parchment.

Lord Trevelin,

I find I must apologize for my piteous behavior when last you called. It is no simple matter to control one's behavior in the face of two deaths in the household, both of which were dreadful blows to me. In Mama's absence, Lady Marlowe was the closest to a mother I had left in the world. I now find myself alone in the house with two widowers, never invited anywhere, and without anyone to escort or sponsor me if I were to receive one. My cousin expected me to eschew going out for at least six months after my mother's death, though I am not certain why I can't. The Season starts in less than three! But that is not why I have written you today. It is Dr. Nuttall. I am concerned for him. I live in fear of the moment you shall come and ask him intrusive and wicked questions that would make him feel as if he is suspected of some dire deed. I plead with you to leave him be.

Sincerely,

Miss Hannah Andersen

There was much about this missive that struck me as odd. I was immediately put in mind of the two backwards-written notes, but I could not say as to why. And then I realized; the word 'can't' had been in all of them. I drew the two notes from my desk drawer and compared them to Miss Andersen's letter. The handwriting was different, though I realized the backwards writing could never look the same as a natural hand. However, each piece of parchment was of the same size and folded in the same manner. These matters of themselves were not much of a clue, but I could not shake the feeling that all three of them were written by someone rather ignorant.

The intent was the same as well; stay away from Marlowe House. I could not help but wonder why Miss Andersen might have written the one sent to Leavitt House. And then I recalled how effective it had been in prompting Mrs. Leavitt to discourage me from calling on Miss Andersen—or anyone else at the house, I presumed. 'Twas to keep me from discovering the truth at Marlowe House, just as Jane suggested.

Rather than question the doctor, I resolved to go straight to the head of the household, Sir Thomas. When I was ushered into his presence, I was surprised to be greeted with the deference a marquis is generally due. My earlier encounters with him seemed to indicate he felt some discomfort when in my presence.

"My lord!" Sir Thomas said, bowing, his voice pitched high as if he were pleased I had deigned to call on him.

"Sir Thomas, may I again express my sorrow over the loss of your wife? It has been a dreadful winter for Marlowe House, has it not?"

He held out his hand, indicating that I should sit in the chair closest to the fire in a room I supposed was set aside for his personal use. The walls were lined with books, there was a desk in the far corner, and a great dog covered most of the exquisite rug spread out before the hearth.

"Are you aware Miss Andersen has believed herself to be in danger?"

He looked taken aback. "Not at all! She is quite safe here, I assure you. I shall not allow any to take advantage of her, if that is a concern. I realize this is now the home of an unmarried man but, yes, indeed, she is quite, quite safe."

"I am grateful for that assurance, but I wonder that you have not requested a female relative to take up residence, for appearances' sake. But that is neither here nor there; she has told me she fears her mother's death was not an accident. That she fears the same person might wish to harm her, even kill her. What may you tell me about this?"

"Nothing! This is the first I have heard of such notions. Whom does she fear has killed her mother?" When I did not immediately reply, his face blanched and his eyes grew wide. "Could my wife have been deprived of her life by the same person?"

"I pray neither of them has been a victim of foul play, but where there is one unwarranted death more often follow. It is only natural Miss Andersen should be fearful. Is there any you can think of who had a reason to kill both Mrs. Andersen and your wife?"

"No!" He shook his head emphatically. "I loved my wife. I did! She was not always easy to get along with, and she was not able to give me children, but I never held that against her."

"Sir Thomas, I assure you I am not here to accuse you." In fact, it had never occurred to me to do so. And yet, one of the dead was his wife. The notion required further thought. "What do you know about Dr. Nuttall?"

His face turned red. "Are you saying that man killed my wife and her cousin?"

"I do not know. However, he is not what he seems." He was handsome, well-to-do, and respected by many. Much like another killer I knew. "I came to learn your impressions of him. Do you know of any reason he might want either of them dead?"

Sir Thomas looked angry. "I do not like that man! I have not been able to say why but he is a thorn in my side, to be sure! It is perhaps the way he looks at Hannah. And, before that, her mother! I always thought he loved her—it would not occur to me he had reason to do away with her." He jerked his head back as if his thoughts surprised him. "Do you suppose it was Hannah he loves, and he was trying to get her mother out of the way?"

"It has crossed my mind, yes."

"But why would he kill my wife?"

"Perhaps she saw something that would indicate he is a killer."

"Of course! I shall have that man barred from my house this very day!" he announced. "I never wanted him here; I only allowed it for the Andersens. Hannah would not hear of having him depart, but I am now quite frightened for her. I do not know what I shall do if she is taken from me."

"What is this?" I asked. "Taken from you? Had you intended on Miss Andersen living with you indefinitely?"

He looked struck, as if he had said too much. "There is nowhere else for her to go. She is a relation. What am I to do?"

I thought his words indicated more than a connection through marriage, but I had no wish to reveal my suspicions. "Do not hesitate to inform me of anything untoward. If Miss Andersen is in danger, it is my wish to help at any cost."

"Indeed, I shall, but I am certain there is no need. I shall keep her safe."

I wondered at his certainty, when two women under his protection had already met their deaths. As I pondered what had transpired, it occurred to me that if Sir Thomas were in love with Hannah, it would be to his benefit to remove both women from existence. Rather than answers I now had more questions and another suspect.

As much as Miss Andersen's situation troubled me, my own was more pressing. The night following my conversation with Sir Thomas, I escorted Jane to a ball. As I waltzed with her in my arms, I posed to her an imaginary situation—a test, if you will, of her resolve. Or her love. (It proved to be a better word for it, after all.)

"Jane," I said, giving her my best smile. "I propose a guessing game of sorts." In my mind, it was more akin to verbal snapdragons, a game in which one must snatch a raisin from a bowl of flaming brandy without suffering burns.

"I suppose that depends on what sort it is," she said, her smile an invitation limited only by my dreams.

We whirled around the room for a few measures whilst I gathered my courage. Finally, there was nothing for it but to forge ahead. "I shall suggest a scenario and attempt to guess what you would do in those circumstances. If I am correct, you suggest one and try to guess what I would do."

"Very well. How does one determine the winner?"

"The one who guesses correctly most often—but one must be honest! Let us say two out of three to start."

"Who shall begin?" she asked, perfectly willing.

"Would it be ungentlemanly for me to insist on going first?"

"I shall forgive you, just this once," she said with a coy look that made my stomach flip.

"Thank you," I said, in a pleasant manner that belied my intentions. "Let me see," I hedged, as if I had not thought on this very subject for days. "Let us make believe your dearest friend and confidante were to suddenly turn cold towards you. Perhaps you are together at a party one night, thoroughly enjoying one another's company, and the next morning she feigns not to know you when you meet by chance at the circulating library. The reason for this treatment is never given. What would you do?"

"Well! I would—" she began, but I stopped her.

"You mustn't say!" I instructed. "I am to deduce what you would do. I believe," I said, my voice wavering with the melancholy I dared not reveal, "you would be terribly hurt. You would feel most forlorn and might never recover from the blow."

She lifted a brow. "I regret to inform you that you have lost the first round."

Despite my fears, I was taken aback. "Have you no sensibilities?" I asked with a mock frown.

"But, of course I do! And they need not be trampled by such a lack of consideration. I would never speak to her again and feel it no great loss. I have no desire to consort with such a person."

"And you would not be hurt?" I asked, still astonished.

"I do not believe I would. Rather, I would consider myself mistaken in esteeming such a person in the first place." She held her nose in the air and dissolved into laughter. "Now," she said, "I believe it to be my turn."

"Indeed," I said, though I felt the game was not proceeding as I wished. "What shall you guess about me?"

"Hmmm, what about this? What if I were to spurn you for another?"

There was no need for her to divine the answer; it was doubtless plainly writ across my face.

"I do believe you would be envious," she teased.

"I cannot deny it," I said, tightening my arms around her.

181

"Perhaps even somewhat injured."

How I wished to show her just how much by pulling her tight against me and branding her with my kiss! Instead, I gave her what I knew to be a hideous frown. "More than you know," I said with a growl meant to convey all that my paltry words dared not.

It was clear she had not the least idea how I suffered. "Well, then, 'tis one point for me! It is again your turn."

Her response to my first scenario was not hopeful. What bitter pill would I be forced to swallow with the second? I drew a deep breath and proceeded with my plan. "What if I were to suffer from a dreaded disease, one I kept a secret from you?"

"What sort of disease? Not leprosy!" she said with a laugh. "One cannot be in doubt of a missing nose."

"Point taken! However, what if I knew I were afflicted but you did not. Naturally you would not wish to contract it yourself. Would you rather I were to break off our betrothal with no word of explanation, ostensibly to protect you from the taint of association, or would you rather I married you anyway in hopes you would not become ill—simply because I loved you too much to give you up?"

"And?" she asked, her beautiful red brows arched in inquiry.

The fact I did not know the answer to this question was the reason for the farce. I vacillated as to how I should respond. She had risked much by becoming my betrothed; she had done even more to rebuild my reputation. She avidly pursued what she wanted, and for some miraculous reason she wanted me. I hoped that if she truly had affection for me, she would make the sacrifice so that we could be together.

And yet, her response was unknowable. I decided to supply the answer I wished for. "I believe you would rather marry me, regardless of anything else; because you are fond of me and would be willing to endure anything for the chance to be together." I smiled my hopefulness. (I was as naïve as any schoolboy in those days.)

She laughed. "Let us just say that it is our good fortune you do not have leprosy!"

I did my best to hide my dismay. "What if you had been my nurse and had once healed me of leprosy. Might you not believe you could heal me again?"

She frowned. "An affliction that has been cured and still returns is not a risk I am willing to take. Clearly it was not wholly cured in the first place. But it is of no consequence, as you do not have leprosy!"

My spirits sank; Eve was an affliction every bit as debilitating as leprosy. "What if I did? Would you rather I told you of it? Or would that put you in an impossible position?" I stared at her intently.

She gazed back at me, suddenly aware there was more at stake than I had let on. "Yes, it would. I suppose I would resent it, too. It would be most gentlemanly to break it off with as little spectacle as possible. I detest melodramatic displays of emotion."

I had my answer, but I had never been so unhappy. Somehow, I managed a merry laugh. "'Tis but a game! I have lost two and you have won merely one. What scenario do you have for me this time?"

"Must we?" she said petulantly. "It is not a very entertaining game, after all." She turned her head, her gaze held by something across the room.

Later, we rode home together, seated side by side. I feared it would be the last time I would be so close to her again. Aware she would likely never be mine, I hesitated to take liberties. Worse, I suspected that once she received my letter ending our betrothal, I would not have the opportunity to bid her a proper goodbye.

I attempted to be content with taking her hand in mine, but she looked up at me, her eyes full of apology, and drew closer. My arm seemed to go around her shoulders of its own volition. Gazing into her marvelous eyes, I committed to memory the way they flashed from jade to emerald in the flickering light of the carriage lamps.

Memories were all I would have left.

Next, I stored away the sprinkling of freckles across her nose. The light dusting of powder she wore could not disguise the fact they were nearly as red as her hair piled high on her head, like a flame. Her nose was tipped upwards, her face unobscured by a bonnet of any kind. Her lips parted as she smiled, and I could not refrain from traversing the silky lengths of them one last time.

'Twas a kiss meant to last a lifetime. If I could not have

her, there would never be another. As I put my mouth to hers, I knew the memory of it must endure 'til the day I died. I paused, allowing my lips to warm against hers, until there was no saying where my flesh ended and hers began. The heat of my passion leapt to life like a flame in a sudden draft. Placing my other arm around her, I gathered her close; so close, I could smell the scent of her rising from her neck. I allowed my lips to stray there as well, allowed my hands to go wherever they willed.

"Julian," she said softly.

I did not, at first, hear her. I was consumed with longing for her and the pathos of our parting.

"Julian!" she said more urgently.

I came to myself and realized I had asked too much of her. "I beg your pardon," I said, aghast. If she knew she would soon find herself without a fiancé, she would be furious with me for the liberties I had taken. "I forgot myself. It was not gentlemanly of me..."

"You are forgiven," she said lightly. "'Tis only that I have no wish to consummate our love in a carriage."

I stared at her, more aghast than before. "Nor do I! I simply failed to refrain . . . I swear it shall not happen again," I murmured, returning my limbs to their proper arrangement and moving across to the seat opposite her.

"Pray, do not be offended Julian, dear. Once we are married, there will be time and enough for kisses," she said with a smile that promised so much more.

Turning from the bright, glorious vision of her, I suppressed a groan. My Jane—she was lost to me forever.

Chapter Sixteen

I spent the following morning attempting to rewrite the letter in which I so coldly cast her aside. After the way I had behaved the night prior, she would never understand the original communication consisting of just three, short lines.

Dear Jane,

It is over. I blame myself. Please do not think on me too unkindly,

Yours, Julian.

Indeed, that would only provoke her. What possible reason would she attach to the withdrawal of my affections? She would believe I spurned her for not allowing me to do as I wished in the carriage, or that I cried off because she allowed me to go as far as I did. I had no wish to add cruel misunderstandings to the pain Eve threatened to have heaped upon her.

In the end I crumpled every new attempt, deciding she had meant what she said; she preferred brevity. As I left my chamber, I thought I heard Willy call after me. "What are you going to do, Trev?" I slammed the door shut behind me, cutting his sentence in half by means of a plank of wood in the jamb. It was time to deal with other correspondence: that of Miss Andersen's.

When I arrived again at Marlowe House, I was astonished to see she still failed to wear black in respect for her mother's and aunt's deaths. However, her grief was real enough.

"You must forgive me, my lord," she said as she entered the palatial front salon where I attempted to warm my fingers and toes by the fire. "Sir Thomas prefers I not closet myself in one of the smaller salons. He wishes to keep an eye on me. Now that he is my sole guardian, he has become quite strict."

"You must feel so alone; isolated, even."

She nodded, her smile tight. "I do understand; he wants what is best for me. Pursuing a marriage match at this point is quite impossible." She seated herself. "He wants me safe whilst I go through the mourning period. As Lady Marlowe was unable to have children, I am his sole heir. I suppose that is something to be grateful for," she said with a sigh.

"How astonishing!" I slid a chair closer to the fire and sat. "I had no idea you might inherit all of this."

"Nor I. It was only after we had been here for some time that Sir Thomas pointed out I should rightly inherit once he and his wife had gone the way of the world." Her tone was sad and steeped in regret.

Puzzled, I posed more questions. "Does he not have a closer relative on his side of the family?"

"Oh, yes! He has a younger brother and a number of nieces and nephews."

"I wonder why he should choose to leave all he has to you rather than to them. Does his brother not think it odd?"

"I do believe he might," she said slowly, "but Sir Thomas explained that they have more than enough. He is anxious on my behalf. I have no prospects. I am not likely to marry well without a dowry."

It would have been far more appropriate for him to provide her with a generous dowry so as to marry her off to a suitable beau. To leave her everything, including the large house in which we sat, seemed too much. I concluded he admired her and hoped to woo her to his side.

Our gazes locked and suddenly she rose to her feet as if to dismiss me.

"I beg your pardon," I dutifully said. "I have no wish to offend you. I shall depart; however, might I first ask you a few more questions?"

"Of course." Her pinched expression belied her words.

It was then I realized I had forgotten to bring the three pieces of parchment with me. I knew I must contrive something else. "Why do you wish that I not question Dr. Nuttall?"

She swallowed and looked down at her hands. "I suppose it is that I care for him. He was so good to my mother, and very kind to me. He has endured such tragic circumstances. I do not believe he deserves to be vexed in any way."

"But you think he might have killed your mother? And wishes to kill you?"

"No! I do not think so," she said with a vehement shake of her head.

"Then, who? You seem unafraid of Sir Thomas. Do you suspect his wife? Have you felt more secure since she died?"

"I..." She blinked rapidly, as if unsure of what to say. "I suppose I felt she had some animosity towards us. You see," she said, taking a chair close to mine and speaking in low tones, "there was a time when Sir Thomas had a *tendre* for my mother. Lady Marlowe resented it."

"When was this?" I asked.

"Oh, a very long time ago. She might even have introduced the woman to Sir Thomas."

"So, your mother was acquainted with him before he met his wife?" I asked to clarify.

"I am not certain of the particulars and now there is no one to ask."

"Save Sir Thomas," I urged.

"Oh, I would not! He is still so sad about his wife's death. Please promise me you shall not harry him!"

"Miss Andersen," I said, as patient as I could be, "you do not wish me to harry Dr. Nuttall, and now you do not wish me to harry Sir Thomas. Is there a reason for this?"

"Only that I feel pity for each of them, and do not wish them to be made to feel a murderer!"

"But you wish me to continue to attempt to discover who has killed your mother? And Lady Marlowe?"

She frowned. "Lady Marlowe tripped on the stairs. My mother could very well have died by accident. I am still here so, as you see, there is nothing about which to ask uncomfortable questions."

I did not agree. "Why did you send Dr. Nuttall after me when I visited the graveyard at Ashford? He was determined to stop me, and he did, indeed."

"Did he?" She smiled, as if pleased in the way one is when a beau has acted on your behalf. "He has not told me of it. But, he did not do so because I wished him to. I merely expressed a desire that you should not wear yourself out on a tiresome journey in the cold to discover my father's burial place. Of what use could it be, anyway?"

"I could not say. I was struck on the head and given a concussion. I never did locate his grave."

She smiled again. "As I predicted it was a pointless journey, one which I am very sorry you were forced to endure. It was wrong of Dr. Nuttall to hurt you, though. I hope he has adequately begged your pardon."

I realized she knew more of the attack in the graveyard than she was willing to admit. "Yes, he did," I said with a faint smile, as I speculated as to why she lied for him. If the physician knew she was to inherit Marlowe House and all that came with it, he would have good reason to endear her to himself. It might even be a motive for murder.

"Were you aware Dr. Nuttall's wife has been found?"

She looked struck. "No! Why has he not gone to her?"

"Sadly, it was her long-dead remains that were discovered. Has he not gone to attend to it, then?"

"He did say he must go home, but not that it had anything to do with his wife. The poor man! He has wondered all these years what had happened to her. Where was she found? How did she die?"

I considered what was proper to reveal to such a young lady and decided the less I said the better. "She became trapped in an unfrequented room of the house where no one heard her cries. Her husband was out of the country at the time. It has taken this long for someone to happen upon her remains." I blinked rapidly to hold my tears at bay. "It must be such a relief for him to finally know what became of her."

Miss Andersen covered her mouth with her hand, tears streaming down her face. "How dreadful! The poor man; I must write to him immediately!"

"Is he not due to return soon?"

"I cannot say. His role was to care for my mother. Now that she is gone, I suppose he shall need to take up his practice again."

"Am I correct to believe you shall miss him?"

She again stood. "As I have said, he has been kind. I thought perhaps, at one time, he was dangerous. However, I have since discovered he wishes nothing but the best for me. In fact, you may consider yourself absolved of attempting to protect me from a killer. I regret asking you. There has never been a need. To fear for my life was but a flight of fancy, one in which I ought not to have indulged. But I do thank you for all you have done—it has brought me some comfort at a difficult time." She held out her hand.

191

Rising, I took it and sketched a slight bow. "I am delighted to know you feel safe and secure. I shall leave you in peace. Please accept my best wishes for you and your future."

She nodded, and I left her behind, for what I thought was forever. However, when I returned home I took out the letters and examined them again. If they were all written by the same person, Miss Andersen had more questions to answer. And then I realized my foolishness. She might not have written any of them, including the one with her signature. Someone else in that house wanted to chase me away and had wished me to believe it was her. Perhaps it was a servant; that would account for the informal grammar. I resolved to take the letters to Miss Andersen in a few days' time, when she had had a chance to recover from my last visit. Perhaps she might help me to discover the truth.

I then turned my attention to the letter I had for Jane. There was nothing for it but to have it delivered. "Jack!" I called. When he appeared, I handed him the carefully sealed missive. Feeling that it was my very heart placed into his hand, I cleared my throat of the lump that had risen therein. "See that this is delivered to Leavitt House in St. James Square." Suddenly I was taken with a fit to see her one more time, before she learned she was no longer wanted. "Ensure it is carried there tonight after nine." I knew she planned to attend a card party at the Radfords', one to which I had declined to accompany her. "Do you understand? It is not to be delivered before that hour."

Jack nodded and took himself off to attend to my wishes. I paced the room until the gong sounded for dinner, surprised Willy did not appear in the meantime. Undecided as to how I ought to feel about seeing Jane again, I ate little. My plan was to wait on the stoop until she came out of the house to board the carriage. What, then, would I say to her? I hoped the words would come to me when the time was right.

When I could bear it no longer, I jumped up from the table and ordered out the carriage. When it finally arrived, I climbed aboard full of anticipation; a mingling of apprehension and excitement. But my eagerness was yet to be satisfied; the journey to Leavitt House never seemed to take as long. I ordered the coachman to stop a block away and I got out to walk the remaining distance. It occurred to me there might yet be a long wait before she appeared. She would most likely still be readying herself for her night out.

I was cutting across the park in the center of the square when I realized that light spilled from her bedroom window on the second floor. I willed my eyes to see through the drapery that adorned the glass, my heart pounding in my chest. I had to see her! Once she had read my letter, she would never look the same to me. Nor would she look on me the same; there was little doubt of that. Panic tightened my throat as I prayed for a miracle.

Heaven's response was swift and sure; the skies opened with a vengeance. The ensuing deluge soaked me to the bone in an instant. As I began to turn away, I caught the swish of fabric at her window. My heart pounded faster now. But it was only a maid who had parted the drapes and peered out, perhaps to assess the weather. When she scurried away without closing them, I dared to hope I might yet get my wish.

I tossed my hat to the ground, heedless of the cascade of water that showered my jacket as it spun away from me. Catching hold of the tree branch just above my head, I swung myself high enough to see into the room. My view included a damask valance that graced the canopy of a bed, and the edge of a carved frame. Closest to the window I could see the ornate top of a floor-length looking glass. Standing perilously on the tips of my toes, I managed to raise my vision enough to take in the top of a head, one of magnificent red hair.

The sudden fall of rain ceased, and the clouds parted, revealing a full moon. It shone on the leaves above my head, and exultant I climbed, ignoring the danger in trusting my weight to branches too small for such a burden. Then, finally, there she was, her countenance beautiful, perfect, full of hope. She gazed into the mirror, ever the coquette. Seducing the glass with her emerald eyes; perhaps even feigning it was me. Overwhelming delight and sorrow filled me with equal force. I thought I would burst from the violence of the battle within my breast.

I do not know how long I might have remained watching the expressions flicker across her face. It was the falling star above the house that drew my attention. It seemed to slash through the sky far too quickly for such a silent endeavor. I felt its turmoil in the center of my being; the death of a superfluity of light. As I gazed up into its dying, I could see that the sky was full of stars. The notion offered no solace. Too many stars had fallen on me.

Climbing down, I lurked in the park until she emerged from the house and boarded the waiting carriage. She put me in mind of Cendrillon, Perrault's heroine who, adorned in finery, boards a magical coach full of hope. The difference was Jane had no warning that on the stroke of midnight she would transform into a young maid with no marriage prospects.

Once the coach had disappeared from view, I separated myself from the shadows. My heart in my shoes, I dragged myself along the street to where my carriage waited. I still cannot recall stepping inside or the journey from there to Silvester House. No Mrs. S. waited inside to distract me. There was only the fire in the green salon and a decanter of brandy to keep me company.

I considered retiring so that I might speak with Willy but was seized with a fear he had gone again. Perhaps for good this time. Finally, I decided it was far more acceptable to drink myself to death where I was than to carry bottles to my bed to do the deed.

As I imbibed, I could not refrain from imagining Jane's reaction when she returned home from the card party and read my missive. It was as if I were fascinated with the horror of it; I could not look away from its painful truth. Knowing she would coldly survive my rejection was that which made me put the glass to my lips again and again. Perhaps, if I had been a different man—a better man—she might have wished her life to end as much as I wished the same for me. The possibility brought little comfort, as there was nothing more unlikely.

I awoke in the morning in my own bed, wondering how I had got there. It was very quiet and quite late in the day; too late to change my mind and recall the letter. Jane was no longer my betrothed, my beloved, or even my friend. She would never forgive me, of this I was certain. Willy did not appear to point out the error in my thinking. I could only assume he knew it was true as well as I did.

With a jolt, I realized there was nothing to keep me in London. I had come for the Frost Fair to please Jane and her parents. I was no longer charged with discovering the truth behind the deaths of either Mr. or Mrs. Andersen. I was free to do as I wished. My country estate was far more comfortable; I might spend entire days on my own with no need to even dress of a morning. Willy had never attended me there. Perhaps he was why I decided to remain in London for as long as I had.

"Good morning, Trev! There has been no rain and the sun has been shining for nearly an hour."

"What has been keeping you?" I asked. "I haven't seen you in days."

"I have been here. You had no wish to see me." He smiled an apology, as if he were the one who had been in the wrong.

I ignored him, fluffing up my pillow to make myself more comfortable. "I have sent Jane a letter."

"Which one?"

I was continually surprised at his wealth of information. As far as I could recall, he had not been in the room when I wrote the missives. "The short one. She has no patience for mewling, or for explanations that might evoke in her a sense of shame. She would prefer the connection between us be dropped clearly and succinctly," I explained, enunciating my words with care.

"How very cold-hearted of her."

I rolled over onto my side and looked out at the sky through the window beyond Willy's head. "Indeed."

"And you? Are you not cut up over losing her?"

"'Tis all I can think of," I said, my voice dull. "Her feelings, her shame, what shall happen to her when the gossip hits the broadsheets. What I shall do without her."

"What *shall* you do?"

I sighed and rolled onto my back. "Who knows? I anticipate I shall once again be very much unwelcome in Society. It is no small thing to jilt a rich debutante."

"You mustn't pretend as if you do not feel sorry for yourself," he cautioned. "Who shall learn who is the killer at Marlowe House?"

I felt myself frown. "*Is* there a killer at Marlowe House?" I turned again to face him. "Is that something you know? Because you are, er, you know..."

"Dead?" He smiled ruefully. "I was at Canning House

and now I am here. I know nothing about the hereafter, if that is what you meant."

"In that case, you are no help at all," I jibed.

Suddenly he was standing next to the bed. "Trev, you must find out who has killed Mrs. Andersen. Who wrote those letters? That is the person you are after."

I stared up into his face, so earnest and kind. "I shall think about it." Then I threw back the covers, got out of bed, remembered to don my dressing gown before opening the door to my chamber, and called for Jack.

When I turned around, Willy was gone. It seemed he had no liking for my boot boy. I went to the basin and washed. When Jack appeared, I was surprised so see how much better his face looked. "It seems a mutton chop has healing properties," I mused, scrutinizing the faint bruise.

He said nothing in response as he went to the clothespress to choose my attire. In fact, there was no conversation between us as he shaved and dressed me like the child that I was. When he had done with me, I went down to the breakfast room and found I had arrived too late. It had all been cleared away. I walked into the front hall to inform a footman I would have toast and coffee on a tray in the salon. Once there, I was unsurprised to find Mrs. S. seated at one of the occasional tables as if in wait of breakfast. Mine.

"Good morning," I said shortly as I dropped onto the divan and went through the morning's correspondence.

"It is late. Are you not sleeping well, my lord?" she

asked as she examined me through the cloudy *Prince nez* affixed to her nose. "You look a trifle wan."

"Who wouldn't appear sickly when viewed through those spectacles?" I asked as I tossed aside the invitations.

She took the lenses and wiped them on her sleeve. "Oh! 'Tis no wonder you were cloudy," she explained.

I bit back a rude retort. "Miss Andersen is still taking advantage of my offer to pay for her wardrobe," I said as I examined the latest dun from her dress-maker.

"You offered to pay for Miss Andersen's clothing?" Mrs. S. asked, properly scandalized.

"Beg pardon—I hadn't meant to say that aloud," I explained as I tossed the bills after the party invitations. Those would doubtless be fewer of those before the week was out.

She blinked at me. "But you did. It was a very compellent comment."

I let out a gusty sigh. "I cannot say whether you found it compelling or repellent. Either way, I have no wish to explain."

"Very well," she said with a tolerant smile. "What shall we do today?"

I stared at her in consternation when, quite suddenly, a thought most compellent occurred to me.

Chapter Seventeen

I leaned forward in my seat and offered Mrs. S. what I hoped was an irresistible smile. "I have yet to discover what is happening behind closed doors at Marlowe House. Perhaps you might agree to assist me."

Her delight was obvious in the color of her cheeks. "Yes! Oh, my, yes! What shall you have me do? I am quite talented. You would not believe it to see me now, I have put on so much flesh, but I excel at crossing a room without a sound."

I had never doubted anything less. "I fear that skill shall not be of any use, Mrs. S. The ground floor at Marlowe House is of marble, not planked. No, I have something else in mind. I need to discover who has written a set of letters. To prove who in the house wrote them, I shall require samples from each of the residents."

"Even Lady Marlowe? That might prove difficult," she mused, planting a pudgy finger to the dimple in the center of her pudgy chin.

"Only the current residents," I explained. "Lady Marlowe's death preceded the letters."

Her face fell. "It is so sad that she has died. But," she said, her fit of melancholy gone as fast as it came, "how are we to acquire writing samples from the others in the house? And what of the servants? Ought we to include them?"

"Only those who know how to write." It was then I realized that any one of them might have paid a scribe or clerk to write them out. 'Twas a wrinkle that would have to wait for another day. I scooped up my mail and rose to my feet. "I shall call for you in a half-hour's time. Shall you be ready by then?"

"How absurd! I am ready as I am!" she insisted.

I took in the head of wispy hair sans hat and the wrapper she donned as the sole guard against the frigid air. "I believe you ought to at least fetch a bonnet and pelisse. We are making a social call, after all."

She sighed as she rose heavily to her feet. "Very well. I shall expect you in a quarter of an hour. I trust that shall be enough time for you to come up with a suitable plan," she said, favoring me with a gimlet stare.

I shared her hope. It would be simple to insist the butler bring the few servants who could write to a room where I might observe the wielding of the quill. It would not help me identify one who paid someone else to write for them, however. Meanwhile, I would need to determine how to acquire samples from Sir Thomas, Miss Andersen, and Dr. Nuttall.

When I rapped upon Mrs. S's front door, I had not decided on anything further. I was startled, however, to see

201

she had dressed as if we were about to board a ship bound for the Arctic. She wore a cap, an item of apparel she usually forgot to don before bringing herself to Silvester House, and a bonnet atop that, as was proper. In addition, she wore the hood of a calash over it all and had tied it tightly under her chin. Nothing under the deep blue cape was visible save a double row of ruching to her skirt and a pair of heavy jean boots more suited to tramping about the countryside. Though it was difficult to find fault with any of the specifics, the overall effect was rather staggering.

Biting my lip before I spoke my observations aloud, I offered my arm for her support and we were soon on our way to Marlowe House.

"What, then, is your plan, my lord?" she asked as she adjusted the voluminous folds of her ensemble along the seat of the carriage.

"You shall provide a distraction," I said, feeling my way through it, "whilst I go above stairs and search the bedchambers for correspondence."

She stared at me as if I were daft. "That shall never serve!"

I opened my mouth to agree with her. How I was to accomplish such without being noticed would doubtless prove impossible, but she interrupted me.

"People do not save the letters they themselves have written. You must look, instead, for diaries, journals. That sort of thing. Though, Lady Marlowe very well might have love letters from her husband. Be sure they are signed, however!" she warned with a finger in my face. "She might have had other sweethearts."

I frowned. "Was she known to have had?" I had learned that no piece of information was too small to have bearing on a murder.

"I haven't the slightest. However," she said, exuberant, "she is the one most likely to possess correspondence from her husband, as well as Miss Andersen, and perhaps even the physician."

I vented a sigh of relief and sat back against the seat with new confidence. I would simply request to meet with the servants in a room on the first floor or above. Mrs. S. would then keep them occupied whilst I went on the hunt for Lady Marlowe's room. It all seemed quite ordinary (for a meddler such as myself) and unexceptionable, and I congratulated myself on a well-thought-out plan. First, however, I must ensure Miss Andersen and her older cousin were out. Dr. Nuttall, I trusted, was still out of town.

I was fortunate; all went as I wished. Sir Thomas had taken Miss Andersen for a drive in the park and the physician was still not in residence. It was then that I took the butler aside. "I hope you can forgive my masquerade last month. My only wish is to ensure the residents of this house are safe." I paused to impress upon him the gravity of the matter. "I have reason to believe someone has deprived Mrs. Andersen of her life."

The butler's sharp black brows came down hard. "By design?"

I nodded. "There are a number of items I shall require. To start with, a room above stairs I may use to question the servants, one in which I shall not be disturbed."

"Very good, my lord. And the lady?"

"She shall remain with me," I said, as if I hadn't just asked for the equivalent of a room in a tavern in which to consort with Mrs. S. "Then, please send up only the servants who know how to write. We shall start with you," I suggested.

"Very good, my lord." He set out across the hall to the staircase and we followed along behind. I could think of one thing only: how relieved I was to be taking a set of stairs in search of a killer in the light of day. Once shown into a room, a guest chamber from all appearances, I ransacked the desk for parchment and a quill. Taking them, along with the inkpot, over to a table, I placed them before the butler, who was most uncomfortable about being seated whilst Mrs. S. and I stood.

"Now, do please write out this sentence for me: *You can't call on me.*"

"Very good, my lord."

I watched carefully as he scratched out the sentence and was interested to note he wrote it wrong. It said: *You cannot call on me.* "That's right, Banner. However, I wish you to use a contraction for the word cannot."

He gazed up at me in surprise. He did as I asked, however.

"That is correct. Now, write it backwards."

His eyebrows rose, but he bent his gaze to the paper and completed the request. It was immediately clear he had not written any of the notes based on his handwriting and his inability to write the contraction without being specifically requested to do so. It was important, though, to go through the entire process so that Mrs. S. might simulate it with the others.

I sent him away with instructions to send up the house-keeper followed by the cook, who I assumed was in the habit of recording her shopping lists and recipes. As soon as the butler's footsteps could no longer be heard through the door, I quietly opened it and slipped out of the room, leaving Mrs. S. to conduct the handwriting experiment.

As I moved down the hall, I opened each door, in search of Lady Marlowe's room. It was tempting to recall the night I had discovered the ghostly chamber of the lady of the house at Nuttall Cottage. Both ladies were now dead, possibly murdered. I pushed the thought ruthlessly aside; it was too much tragedy added to my own melancholy circumstances.

Finally I found what appeared to be the room of a married woman of middle age. The luxurious draperies and carpet were slightly faded, as if the room had been lived in for some time. Many of the items I saw were of too recent manufacture for the chamber to have been long out of use, as well. There was only one way to be certain: find something that undoubtedly belonged to Lady Marlowe. I went first to the desk and pulled out a sheaf of parchment tied with ribbon.

On the top was a letter from Mrs. Andersen. In it she thanked her cousin for housing them in advance of the coming Season. It was impossible for the dead woman to have written any of the three notes I had in my possession, but I slipped the letter between my waistcoat and shirt anyway.

There was nothing else of interest in the desk, so I moved on to the chest of drawers. Quickly, I pawed through Lady Marlowe's clothing. Each piece was wrapped in silver tissue until they would be worn again. It called to mind the sense of breathless waiting in Mrs. Nuttall's room and I found I could not keep my mind on my search. The feel of the silks and satins against my skin prompted a deep regret for so many losses. Mrs. Nuttall, gone. Mrs. Andersen, gone. Lady Marlowe, gone. Jane—gone.

Overwhelmed with sadness, I fought against giving up in despair. Then I felt it; something quite different than the smooth, soft materials that filled the drawers. Drawing it forth, I realized it was a thin book, one in which Lady Marlowe had recorded her appointments and other engagements. Leafing through it, I could see that her notations included the day the Andersens were meant to arrive, the day we had all been at the Mackleys' ball, and other insignificant entries.

Placed between the cover and the first page was a small piece of parchment upon which was written a message. It read: *My dearest, you must not allow it to trouble you. Though she is the mother of my only living child, I no longer feel for her what I once did. You are my wife and the love of my life. Never forget that. Yours, T.*

There was no date. However, it seemed not to have any age to it—it might have been written only the day prior. It was an odd sort of message; clearly it was in answer to a letter of hers or even a conversation she and Sir Thomas might have had. It felt pertinent and important, not something that referred to a situation from the long-ago past. I wondered who this child might be and where lived the mother.

And then I knew: Hannah Andersen. She had mentioned her mother and Sir Thomas had been fond of one another and that it was she who had introduced Lady Marlowe to her husband. Perhaps it was she who had helped her cousin through the travails of becoming enceinte with the child of a man to whom one was not wed. I wondered how long after her assignation with Sir Thomas that Mrs. Andersen had married her husband. Had he known Hannah was not his child?

Quickly, I inspected the handwriting and knew it was not the same as seen on the three letters in my possession. I hadn't the chance to look for anything else; however, someone was coming. I added the note to the other in my pocket, returned the book to its place, and carefully closed the drawer. Then I went soundlessly to the door and put my ear against it. It opened so quickly I was forced to leap out of its way.

To my relief, no one entered. I heard a woman say,

"Leave that room for another time. It is no longer in use."
The door was then pulled shut and a pair of footsteps
receded towards another door. I opened mine and peeked
down the passage, to see someone disappear into a
bedchamber. Making my escape to the room where I had left
Mrs. S., I discovered it was quite empty. I now needed to
learn what had become of her, and without being seen.

I stepped out again into the passage and was
immediately confronted with the astonished countenance of
Dr. Nuttall.

"What is the meaning of this?" he demanded. "How are
you in my chamber?"

I could not decide which caused me the most chagrin;
that I had been caught out by the physician or that I had
been in his room and had not searched it. I drew myself up
so that I stood at my greatest height. "Did I not inform you I
have been attempting to discover the truth behind Mrs.
Andersen's death?"

"And you found it necessary to search my things?"

He was angry, to be sure, but of most interest to me was
that he did not insist Mrs. Andersen's death was entirely
natural. "I beg your pardon; is this your room? 'Tis the one
Banner gave me for my use. It was understood you had
departed for Nuttall Cottage with no plans to return."

His demeanor softened. "Do you stay here, then?"

"No. You are quite welcome to it. Again, I beg pardon
for the trespass."

"Good day to you," he said with a nod as he brushed
past me.

I caught his arm as he passed. "Wait!"

He paused, and we stood eyeing one another. He appeared to be as suspicious of me as I was of him. We had something else in common; we had each recently observed the piteous remains of a beautiful, vibrant woman. His patent sorrow was more than I could bear, and I dropped my gaze. "I am sorry for the loss of your wife. I was told you had thought her merely missing and had hopes of one day discovering her whereabouts."

His eyes turned bright with tears, but he gave me a creditable bow. "Thank you. I am sorry to have stood in your way. I shan't again."

"May I ask why not? Do you believe there is a killer in this house?"

He stared directly into my eyes, as if willing me to perceive what was in his mind. "I do not know," he said finally. "I pray not. And yet, I cannot entirely reject the possibility."

"Nor can I. Tell me, whom do you suspect?" I demanded, but he shook his head and, pulling the door open, disappeared inside.

With little choice but to descend to the ground floor, I soon arrived in the front hall. Mrs. S. was nowhere to be seen. I heard her voice, though, as if coming from the small salon where I had met with Miss Andersen twice before. As I entered, I was astonished to find her conversing with Sir Thomas. She was doing an admirable job of comforting him in his sorrow and he seemed to enjoy every moment of it.

"Mrs. Smurthwaite, how good of you to wait here for me."

She looked up in a surprise not one whit less than Sir Thomas'.

"I beg your pardon, Sir Thomas, but I had some business with the physician. I was shown into his room and have been awaiting him there."

"What a stroke of luck! We did not know he planned to return until he showed up here not fifteen minutes ago," Sir Thomas blustered.

I smiled widely. (It was my most innocent expression.) "I count myself fortunate, then. Mrs. S." I said, turning to her, "I must be on my way. May I offer you a ride home or does your carriage wait?"

She looked profoundly confused but, to her credit, quickly rallied. "I sent it away, as I did not know how long I would be. I should be happy to ride home with you, my lord!"

I held out my arm, and with a nod for Sir Thomas, we made our way to the door which was thrown wide for us by the ever-discreet Banner. I did not breathe a sigh of relief until we were in the carriage and it had driven off. "That was a near disaster!" I said.

"Yes, but it was all very effervescent. I have here the samples for the butler, the housekeeper, and the cook. There was also a maid who could write—this is her sample," she said, handing them over to me with the maid's on top.

Taking the pile of parchment, I thanked her. "You have

been marvelous, but I have my own news to share. I was able to view a sample of Sir Thomas' writing."

"Then we have all but Miss Andersen's and Dr. Nuttall's. Unless you managed that as well," she said with a confident smile.

"No," I said ruefully. "I am afraid I wasted the perfect opportunity to search his room."

Mrs. S. continued to smile smugly. "I was most ingenuous," she said proudly. "When the physician came through the door, I was already entertaining Sir Thomas in the salon. I invited him to join us."

"Yes, ingenuous or ingenious, if it yielded results I must hear about it," I insisted, intent on learning what this had to do with a writing sample.

"Well!" she said, equally intent in drawing out the moment of her triumph. "I prevailed upon him for an inscription for headache powder."

"Yes?" I asked, with a great dearth of imagination.

She slipped a piece of parchment onto my lap. "His handwriting!"

Crowing with delight, I caught up the piece of parchment and held it aloft. "Mrs. S., you are ingenious, indeed!" Gathering the scraps of parchment into one bundle, I returned them all to my pocket. "I shall scrutinize them at length when I may compare them to the letters I have at home."

"Very well," she warned, "but I shall wish to know the results of our inspectigations as soon as may be!"

"You have my word, Mrs. S.!" And I meant it, too. However, when I found myself again in the green salon with the brandy decanter at hand, I found I could think of nothing but Jane. My enthusiasm for the pursuit of a killer was merely a way to deaden the pain. Once again, I drank myself into oblivion.

Chapter Eighteen

Come the dawn, I was miserable and crotchety. My head ached, and every move Jack made in riddling the fire caused it to throb. "The reason I keep you," I complained into my pillow, "is because you are far quieter than the maids who used to start the fire of a morning. Be warned!"

I did not hear him again, though I was more than a little aware of the flood of light that entered the room when he threw back the curtains. I dragged my pillow from beneath my head and placed it over my beleaguered eyes. I remained thusly for quite some time. And then I remembered Jane.

"Jack!" I called as I struggled from the bedclothes that had me entangled. "Jack! Where are you?"

He entered the room and stood at the foot of my bed.

"Have I any letters this morning?"

"Yes."

"Very well, then. Fetch them."

He took an unaccountable long time about it. Whilst I waited I took care of my morning ablutions and donned a clean shirt. Pulling on my pantaloons from the night prior, I seated myself at my writing desk.

Finally, he reappeared and handed me the packet of correspondence. I flipped through it, casting each one aside until I had come to the last. "Is that all of it?"

"Yes."

"Go ask Hatch. In fact, tell him I wish to see him here this very moment!"

Jack turned on his heel with no word of complaint, but I thought I heard a sigh as he left. And then I turned to the window and realized it was Willy.

"You are too hard on the boy. 'Tis not his fault Jane has not written."

"Who says she has not?" I demanded.

"Have you had a letter from her?"

"Not yet. But surely Hatch has one somewhere. He is merely holding it back to torment me, much as he does when he allows Mrs. S. to wander the halls of my home."

"She must be dreadfully hurt and more than a little angry. From what you have said, it seems unlikely she shall write. You know I am correct."

I dropped my head into my hands and pulled at my hair. "How could I have done it? I ought to have gone to her, explained all, and then eloped with her. At the very least, I might have acquired a special license and married her out of hand."

"You very well might have done. But you had no wish to put Jane through a period of ostracizing like the one you have experienced. What's more, without her influence and that of her friends, you might be as unacceptable as you were after the duel," Willy mused.

"But why?" I asked as I leapt to my feet. "People from every segment of society consort with those who are not their espoused husband or wife! Why hold me to a different standard?"

"The duke is vengeful, and so is your cousin. They have their reasons."

I sat on the corner of my bed and looked directly into Willy's eyes. "Do you know the reasons? Do you hide the truth from me, or are you as ignorant as I am?"

He spread wide his hands. "Trev, I would never keep anything from you, of that you may be certain."

"That is a comfort at least," I murmured. I held my hand out to shake his but remembered in time that I had no wish to learn how felt the flesh of a phantom.

It was then that Hatch scratched at the door. "Enter," I said, then remembered Willy. I needn't have given him a thought—he was gone. "Hatch," I said heartily as he stood waiting. "I believe some of my correspondence has gone missing. Do a search. Oh," I said, turning again to my mail, "when you have executed that duty, you are dismissed."

"Dismissed, my lord?" he asked, in what sounded to be genuine puzzlement. "For having executed your instructions? I do not rightly understand."

"From my household. For dereliction of duty." I looked up and offered him a cold smile; the one some describe as a sneer.

His face flamed red, but he retained the appropriate demeanor. "Very good, my lord. And am I to continue the search for the gold ring?"

I did my best to keep the chagrin from my face. "There is no need," I said lightly and turned away. I assume he left, but he had already given me too much to think about to give him further heed. In truth, his question struck me hard. I had been wrong to assume any in my household had taken my ring. Perhaps I was as wrong to assume Hatch held back my mail. I had been wrong about Jane, as well; never would I have believed she would have nothing to say to my jilting of her. Perhaps she was merely biding her time in the assumption I would change my mind.

Disheartened I went down to breakfast to find Mrs. S. sitting at my table, eating my kippers, deeply absorbed with the news of the morning paper. "Ahem!" I said to announce my presence. I thought she would be shocked and perhaps a trifle shamed to see me. As usual, she surprised me.

"My lord, I have been waiting for you this hour! Have you read the news?"

I stifled a sigh and went to the sideboard. "Mrs. S., 'tis too early in the day for conversation." I paused to fill my plate. "I am persuaded there is no news that shall not sound better once my hunger is appeased."

"Then you have *not* heard," she proclaimed in a voice of doom.

Dismayed, I turned from the sideboard to see she had somehow managed to push back her chair in utter silence and was now stealing from the room. "Pray forgive me for my rudeness, Mrs. S."

She paused and gave me a sad smile. "I do believe you are correct; you ought to have, at the very least, a cup of good, strong coffee before you read the perilitacals."

"Why? What is it?" I abandoned my plate and took up the papers.

"Good morning to you!" she said, nearly frantic as she took herself off faster than I knew possible for a woman of her age and girth.

Puzzled, I began to read the page she had left open to my view.

It has recently been announced that the heiress Miss L. is betrothed to Lord T. However, Mr. R.R. doubtless has something to say to that arrangement. It has been revealed that he and Miss L. have enjoyed an arrangement of their own. It is high time Lord T. found himself a lady without prior attachments.

Thoroughly aghast, I allowed the paper to slip from my fingers. There are no words to describe the sense of betrayal I felt. To know that Jane was ruined because of the hatred the man bore for me—for *me*—was unsupportable. A hundred thoughts ran through my mind, foremost of all was this: that had she never taken notice of me, felt drawn to me, pitied or admired me, she would be happily preparing for a wedding to another. Someone more suitable. Someone worthy.

I had ruined her as surely as if I had done the deed myself. As such, I was unworthy of her. My fate was to be forever denied all that I longed for: love, happiness, a family of my own to love me and care for me as I yearned to love and care for them.

Then came the most despicable truth of all. There was now no one who would dare to rescue Jane from a loveless life of spinsterhood—unless it was Evelyn Rogers-Reimann.

I bolted from the room and up the stairs to find the ring he had given me—the one that had celebrated my heroic bravery, that had signified his esteem for me as well as my worthiness of that esteem, and from any man or woman. Finding it, I jammed it onto my finger, determined to never remove it, to never forget how little I deserved any of it. I had saved his life, yes, but had broken the dueling code to do so. All along he was laughing at me, at my *naiveté* for believing I had done something extraordinary. That he loved me for it. Even when I had tired of him and his antics, even when all of Society despised me, I always knew that there was one person who believed me to be a hero. And now I knew it was simply a sadistic joke.

In that moment I vowed to never be separated from the ring. I would wear it always as a reminder of who I truly was. Not a hero, but a monster; one who destroyed everyone with whom he came in contact. It didn't matter that I had no intention of hurting a single soul, or that it was not my actions that had done the harm. And yet...clearly, there was something deeply and irrevocably wrong with me. I could not afford to forget it lest it again subject me to such agonizing pain.

My thoughts continued along at a rapid rate. I realized

there would be times when openly wearing the ring would not be appropriate. There would also likely be circumstances in which I preferred to hide my shame away. In such cases I would need a special pocket in which to secrete the ring, one placed such that I could yet feel its cold, hard presence. The waistband of my pantaloons seemed the perfect solution. Pulling open the clothespress, I jerked every pair from its peg. I had just taken the lot of them up in my arms when Jack entered the room.

"Wot?" Taciturn as always, his expression said so much more.

"I am taking these to the tailors; move out of the way."

For a moment he looked as if he would ask a great number of questions. Instead, he took the bundle from my arms and headed out the door. I followed along, my legs columns of sand that shed precious grains with every step. I feared they would utterly fail me, but down the passageway they went, down the stairs behind Jack, who managed the bundle well enough on his own.

Once we were on our way, we must have made an alarming sight. Me, standing upright in the curricle, whipping the horses like a madman; Jack almost buried under a greater number of trousers to which any man is entitled, the curricle careening around corners and flying along the straightaways as if they were race courses.

At the last moment I decided it best to patronize a tailor who was not in the midst of preparing my wedding clothes. I would needs must deal with my usual tailor at a later date, but preferred not to think about it for the time being. Jack stood in the corner of the shop whilst I, my voice shaking with grief and rage, explained what I wished to have done. The ring was measured to ensure there would be enough room for it inside the pocket under discussion. It was decided 'twould be best to place it to the side where my hip bone met my waist. As such, the line of my jacket would disguise any telltale lump. I knew it would be better felt there, as well. Every time I took a step, that lump of gold would remind me of exactly who I was. A worthless failure.

I felt somewhat recovered when we sat again in the carriage headed for home. I had removed the possibility of being dealt such a blow ever again—I would never forget my place, my disgrace, or my lack of worth. Never again would I expect a young lady to smile on me with favor. Never again would I hope for a child to whom I would leave my title, my possessions and holdings; my fortune. As I tooled the carriage, I pictured myself returning to Silvester House in triumph. Had I not controlled my fate and precluded further pain and humiliation? Instead, I found myself turning into an alley, staring at the loops of leather in my hands. The horses were restive and jittery, and it took me some time to realize that Jack was quietly weeping.

I turned to him in surprise. "What is it? Has somebody died? Is it your sister? Is she ill?"

He shook his head fiercely, tears flying from the tip of his nose. "You're goin' to git rid of me, ain't ya?"

"What? No! Why would you think so?"

He sniffed and rubbed his wrist along the bottom of his nose. "I don' know. It's jus' tha' you don' like that tailor. You said you wou' never go to 'im."

I flicked the reins, turned the equipage about, and drove in silence for some time before I replied. "There will be some changes in the coming weeks and months, this is true. However, you shall be present to observe them all."

He nodded, and the color returned to his face.

My heart burned with the knowledge that here was one human being who would never betray or leave me. I felt it another tragedy that he hadn't the right to become the Marquis of Trevelin. He was the closest to a son I was likely ever to have.

That afternoon I found myself once again reaching for a bottle of Dutch courage. I progressed rapidly from brandy to Blue Ruin. As I tilted the azure bottle into my glass, I saw my future hanging in the balance. With a flash of rare insight, I decided I had had enough of feeling sorry for myself. Furthermore, I had a killer to pursue. I went upstairs and pulled the packet of parchment out of the drawer where I had tossed it and compared the handwriting of each with the three letters I already had. There was no match.

I returned to Marlowe House for the second time in two days. As before, I waited for Miss Andersen in the small salon. I wondered what had happened to her cousin's desire that she meet with me in the cavernous reception room where she was safer with reprobates such as myself. When she appeared she looked very tired, as if the trouble in the house was finally catching up to her.

"Good day, Miss Andersen. I pray I do not unduly disturb you. It is only that there is a matter that can be more readily resolved with your assistance."

She folded her hands neatly in her lap. "Of course, my lord."

I held out the letter signed with her name. "'Tis an odd question, but a needful one. Did you write this yourself, with your own hand?"

Her expression hardened, as if she was wounded past bearing. "But of course. I know how to write, my lord! Is there anything in my demeanor or my words that would lead you to believe I am ignorant?"

"Not at all! I am fully aware you are an intelligent, educated young woman. It is only that I have in my possession several other letters that bear similarities. They, however, are not signed. I am wondering if perhaps they were written by you, as well."

She turned white, but she offered me a brave smile. "I do not write many letters, my lord. That being said, my longhand is quite ordinary, much like anyone else's."

"I concede it is possible these three letters were written by different people, despite the parchment being of the same size and folded in much the same way. Two are brief and written backwards, an unusual circumstance to be sure. But there is something else I cannot so easily explain."

"Oh?" she asked, her chin lifted haughtily. "I am sure I do not know the answer to that."

"But you do admit to writing this one?"

"Why should I deny it?" she asked, impatient. "I have signed it!"

"Very good, we are agreed on that point. May I bring to your attention the fact that you have used a contraction for the word cannot? I hesitate to wound you, but it is unusual for a proper lady to use a contraction in speech, let alone in a letter."

She smiled again, her chin quivering. "May I see it, please?" She took it from me and inspected it. "Yes, I see the word to which you refer. I do not see how it signifies."

"By itself, it does not. However, the same thing has occurred in each of these other two letters." I handed them to her.

She studied them as tears started in her eyes. Finally, her hand shaking, she allowed the letters to fall from her fingers and rustle to the floor. "You know."

"I know you wrote each of those letters. What I do not know is why. Do you attempt to protect Dr. Nuttall?"

"No!" She looked wild with worry. "That is, there is nothing of which he is guilty. He is a good man and entirely innocent. He has suffered enough, has he not?" she beseeched. "That is why I wrote the letters; I had no wish for him to be falsely accused and possibly punished for something that was not his doing."

I could feel my heart soften towards her. Sitting next to her, I took her hand in mine. "Miss Andersen is there something you would like to tell me?"

She let out a sound that was half sob and half laughter.

"No, I do not! And yet, I think I must." She turned towards me and looked directly into my eyes. "I killed my mother."

I was taken aback despite my suspicions of the same. "May I ask why?" I said as gently as I knew how.

She vented a sigh. "I resolved never to speak of it to anyone, but I cannot allow Dr. Nuttall to suffer. You know, of course, his wife has been found. He is terribly cut up about it. 'Tis a dreadful business. My desire to save him is greater, I suppose, than my wish to keep my secret."

"I commend you for your decision." At that moment I began to believe she was protecting him, after all.

"It was an accident; there is no doubt of that. I had no reason to wish my mother dead. I loved her deeply! She was my dearest friend and I depended on her for everything!"

"She was often sickly. Did you not tire of it?" I suggested.

"Not at all! We have always lived very quietly, but when she was sick we had many more visitors. People spoke to me, they who would otherwise have no reason to even notice me. Neighbors came by with gifts of food. In some ways, it was more pleasant when Mama was sick than when she was not."

I squeezed her hand in sympathy. "What happened?"

She shrugged. "I merely administered too much medicine. At least, I assume so. It cannot be proved, but her death came so swiftly afterwards that I must believe it was so. I have been living in dreadful agony ever since. But I was a coward!" she cried, as if that were worse than being a killer. "I could not bring myself to tell the truth, even when you were so kind to me that day we spoke of medicines and poisons."

"Yes, I see." We sat together in silence while I considered. "Why, then, did you ask for my help; suggest that you were next?"

"To prevent anyone from suspecting the truth, of course! I did not think, at first, how it might concern Dr. Nuttall. I thought only of myself. I was so very distraught. I had just lost my mother..." she said, wiping at her tears.

I rose to my feet. "I understand."

She looked at me in relief and astonishment. "You do? Is it possible?"

"Yes, indeed. I am sorry you have suffered so greatly and needlessly. If you had told me the truth from the beginning, I would have been able to assure you far sooner."

"I need fear no reprisals?" she asked, breathlessly.

"You have lost your mother, by accident, and by your own hand. I deem that reprisal enough, do you not?"

Quickly she dropped her head and brought her handkerchief to her eyes. "Thank you, my lord," she said, her voice muffled. "You are very kind."

"Now, I urge you to inform Sir Thomas of what you have told me. It shall relieve his mind, I have no doubt."

She nodded. "Yes, yes of course."

I sketched her a bow, though she likely did not see it through the muslin and lace she held to her eyes. I began to walk from the room, and then I turned and asked, "How much medicine did you give her? Was she improving? Was that what troubled you? Did you find it needful to give her more in order to bring on symptoms of which others would take notice? You have admitted you enjoyed the attention it rendered."

She lifted her face from the handkerchief and stared at me, her mouth open but wordless.

Her lack of defense prompted other questions. "How long have you known you are Sir Thomas' daughter? Did you push Lady Marlowe to her death because she knew you had killed your mother, or was it because you have been too long without a father and wished to have him all to yourself?"

Chapter Nineteen

She rose majestically to her feet, her back straight as a board, her face crimson-red, head held high. "Get out!" she cried. "Get out and never return!"

I touched my hat and left. As I climbed aboard the carriage, I was completely numb. I had never sustained so many shocking surprises in so short a time. It was as if I were no longer capable of feeling anything at all. Briefly, my mind touched on my sadness about Jane, but it skittered away again to the matter of Miss Andersen who was, in my estimation, possibly as callous a killer as those responsible for Johnny Gilbert's death.

I returned to Silvester House unsure of what direction to pursue next. I found I was weary of death, and that I had no wish to ensure Miss Andersen be punished. I hadn't any proof, besides. What's more, due to the rumors that were soon to fly about, London would now be intolerable. I had only come to be with Jane; the cold, short days of winter were better endured in the country. More than that, watching Jane's star fall to the pit dwelt in by Evelyn Rogers-

Reimann would be a torment. I could not remain to watch it happen.

I informed Hatch, despite my contempt of him, to prepare the household for departure first thing in the morning. 'Twas only he, Cook, a pair of footmen, several maids, the coachman, and Jack, but 'twould take the better part of a day to make ready. I could be on my way to my country estate, Alders, the next morning or the one after, should the weather hold.

Determined to play the hermit from that moment on, I donned my dressing gown and slippers. Whichever decanter in the green salon that yet contained liquid refreshment was my intended companion for the balance of the evening. We were getting along very well together when Hatch entered, announced I had a visitor, and asked if I were "in".

"I am out," I said, more than a little drunk, "unless, of course, it is Mrs. Smurthwaite at the door, in which case I am in as always."

Hatch stared at me as if he thought me deranged.

"Is that not how it goes? You say I am in whether I wish to entertain her or not?"

"It is Sir Thomas. He is most wishful of speaking with you on a matter most urgent."

"Has another poor soul met with an accident at Marlowe House?" I asked, brandishing my glass.

"I could not say, my lord."

If I had been less inebriated, I would most likely have wished to avoid him. The affable altitudes I enjoyed at the moment, however, rendered me reckless. "Very well! Allow him to enter!"

Hatch withdrew. Whilst I waited for Sir Thomas to appear, I had the presence of mind to hide away the empty bottles before again making myself comfortable on the divan. However, the expression on his face when he entered was not in the least relaxing.

"Sir Thomas, what has happened?"

He bowed deeply and took up a seat. "It is Hannah—that is, Miss Andersen." He averted my gaze and shifted his feet. "She is most distraught. I fear she shall do something dire."

"What has that to do with me?" I asked, despite knowing the answer very well, indeed.

"Nothing! That is, I believe you called on her today, though it is not I who accuses you."

"Am I to understand Miss Andersen accuses me, then?"

He began to cow under my unrelenting gaze. "I only wish to know how best to help her. Perhaps you might shed some light on the conversation between the two of you."

Hatch entered with a tray of tea and cakes, which I instantly fell upon. When I had taken all I wanted, I leaned back against the cushions. With a cup of steaming tea in one hand and a plate of various sweets in the other, I was better prepared to listen. "What has she said about it?"

"That is why I have come to speak with you. She is...most dear to me and I wish to help her if I may. She has had enough with which to cope."

229

I licked sticky crumbs from my thumb and nodded. "Indeed, she has. And you, being her natural father, have every right to ease her way."

His mouth fell open in surprise. "How did you know?"

"She is very much like you," I said by way of evading the question. I had no wish for him to learn I had searched the room of his dead wife. "How long have you known she is your daughter?"

"Her mother informed me at Christmas. I believe she thought it would be a welcome gift for the holiday."

"And was it?" I bit into a scone. "See here, you must have one; the curd is excellent!"

He shook his head. "It was a shock, to be sure, but once I warmed to the idea I was delighted. My wife always knew of it, or so I suppose, but she had no wish for me to be availed of the truth. As such, it was difficult to enjoy my daughter with my wife as witness."

"And your daughter. How did she feel about it?"

"She knew of it before I did. I assume her mother told her. She and I have not discussed it directly. However, I overheard a conversation between her and my wife that reveals her feelings. At the time, I did not know the truth, so I found the exchange puzzling. I know better, now."

"Might you share it with me?"

"Yes, I suppose so," he said, though I could see he was reluctant. "She said her father was a coward and it was time she had one of whom she could be proud. I thought perhaps she referred to Dr. Nuttall, who very much wished to marry

Hannah's mother. He could not, however, as he yet hoped his wife would turn up alive."

I was not surprised. I had almost entirely absolved Dr. Nuttall of murdering his wife. "You did not, at the time, know she referred to you."

He nodded. "That is correct. What I thought odd was how much she liked the notion of me as her father. She has always been incredibly defensive of whom she believed to be her papa. She was insistent that he did not kill himself."

"Perhaps she was ashamed of him, and she felt his cowardice a reflection on herself."

"'Tis not unlikely. Having been raised in a military fort in a foreign country, her entire world was the military. What her father did was, from the perspective of a parent, completely natural. It is a new notion for me, but one I have come to embrace in a very short period of time. I would do anything to protect her! But, according to the military code, it was beyond the pale for him to put the safety of his family before his duty. Even as a small girl, she would have known that."

I sighed, replete, and allowed myself to sink further into the cushions. "Miss Andersen is a beautiful, intelligent young lady. Her efforts to be refined are a credit to her. I fear I am to blame for her current distress. She admitted to me that she killed her mother—quite accidentally—by administering too much medicine. 'Twas a difficult conversation."

His face turned red with anger. "But why? Why would either of you discuss such a matter!"

"I believe she wished me to stop investigating Dr. Nuttall as a murderer. She feels he has endured enough."

Sir Thomas harrumphed. "I am most sorry to learn she has said such a thing. Hannah has been dosing her mother for years. It is highly unlikely she would poison her accidentally."

I felt astonishment. "You believe she knew what it was she did?"

"Of course, not! The woman was always sick; had always been sick. Whatever it was she suffered from finally did her in; that is all."

"Was she sick when you first knew her?"

He looked away. "Not as she was when we met again this autumn. She was young and beautiful, much like Hannah is now. I am very sorry she is gone and that she endured such a difficult life. It has not been easy. They have been treated poorly on account of how her husband met his end."

"I am sorry, as well. 'Tis a dreadful story." I had a thought. "Do you know where he is buried?" I waited eagerly for his response. I had wondered too long if he had been laid to rest with those who had taken the matter of their deaths into their own hands.

"It is my understanding his body was never recovered."

I frowned. "Do you mean to say his remains are at the bottom of a ravine in Africa?"

"I believe so, yes."

"Why would Miss Andersen claim him to have been buried in England?"

"Perhaps her mother told her so. She was quite young. Or perhaps it was to minimize the shame. He died a coward's death, and that is not something she could tolerate."

"Yes, I see," I murmured.

Sir Thomas rose. "I believe I have had my question answered. I thank you for your candor."

"Of course. Perhaps you would do the same for me. I find I must ask how your wife died."

He bristled. "'Twas an accident! She caught her heel on the hem of her gown and fell to the marble below." His eyes filled with tears.

"Were you a witness to this accident?"

"No. I was out."

"May I ask who was present at the time?"

"I don't rightly know. Hannah is the one who found her, however. What a terrible ordeal! 'Twas she who found her mother dead as well!"

"Hmmm, that does not surprise me. Was anyone else at home at the time, besides Miss Andersen and the servants?"

"I do not believe so. Why do you ask?" He frowned.

"'Tis nothing. Only, like you said, it must have been difficult. Three accidental deaths in her family is a heavy burden to bear."

"Yes, well," he said, clearing his throat. "She is a dear

girl; all that I have left. I believe I shall collect her and take her to Gunter's for an ice."

"An excellent notion. I must bid you goodbye. I depart tomorrow for the country. Please give your daughter my compliments."

His cheeks turned pink as he smiled. "I will. I will, indeed!" He bowed and departed before I could change my mind and tell him what I really thought of his daughter.

Once Sir Thomas had gone, Hatch reappeared to remove the tea tray.

"Is all being readied for our departure tomorrow morning?" I asked.

"If you wish, my lord," he said, the lid in the teapot rattling as he went.

"Wait! I have just recalled that my pantaloons are at the tailor's. We shall have to delay until those can be collected. Send one of the footmen 'round first thing in the morning to see if they are ready."

"Yes, my lord."

I vented a final sigh of relief when the door shut behind my butler. He had been with the family all my life, but he had never liked me. Matters had become worse after the duel. And yet, aside from the matter of allowing entrance to those I had no wish to see, he did as I asked.

Later, when I went above stairs to retire, Jack was in my room brushing crumbs from my coat and collecting spent neck cloths.

"Have you been told? We are to retire to Alders in a day or two."

He merely nodded, but I could see that he was pleased.

"Do not say you have a girl in Sussex!" I teased him.

He gave me a scathing look. "I'm four'een."

"Is that too young to court a young lady, then?" I had become a marquis when I was only a year older.

"No. I don' know." He stopped what he was doing to look at me. "We shou' stay put."

"At Alders, you mean?" I laughed. "So you *do* have a young lady."

"Din' say so. It's jes'...She ain' righ' for you."

There was a moment of stunned silence that had little to do with the inappropriateness of such a discussion between a valet and his master. I turned to the mirror, feigning interest in the cleanliness of my teeth. "I believe you refer to Miss Jane Leavitt."

"Yes," he whispered.

"You need have no fear on that score. I have broken our betrothal."

I could feel his mood lighten. "Ya did?"

"She was of a mind to dismiss you as my valet and demote you to boot boy. I could have none of that, so, piff! She's gone." I turned around to face him. "Now, I expect my pantaloons to appear sometime tomorrow. I shall wish to inspect them before they are packed."

"Yes, sir!" He practically danced from the room.

I reflected for a moment on why he disliked Jane—he hadn't known until now she wished to dismiss him.

"'Tis because he knows she cannot make you happy."

I turned to face Willy. "How could he possibly know such a thing?"

"How does anyone know anything when it comes to love?"

"But he has not so much as met her."

"He has met you when you have been with her."

"I am no different! Rather, I am better."

We were interrupted in our discourse by a rap upon the door. It was a footman with a note. Opening it, I reported its contents to Willy. "Walter has finally produced the name and direction of the woman Dr. Nuttall abandoned when he met Mrs. Andersen." I turned to see my companion's reaction, but he was gone.

I set out the next morning to pay a call on one Miss Mary Swinton. Her address was located near the docks on the east side of the city. Crime was a way of life in such a place, and I gripped my concealed blade tightly in my hand. As I stepped out of the carriage I had an uncanny feeling, as if someone were gazing down at me. I was accustomed to being spied upon from an upper room, so that the lady of the house could determine whether she wished to receive me. This, however, felt different; far more unfriendly, even sinister.

It was with some trepidation that I rapped upon the door. I was yet questioning my choice when it opened, and I was admitted by a short, spotty-faced footman; 'twas not at all the thing. My enthusiasm waned utterly when I was shown into a second-floor salon, one at the back of the house with a view of the mews. A slight odor of decay rose from the street despite the fact the windows were tightly shut. The day was cloudy and the room dark; I barely made out the shape of a woman in a gray gown seated in a corner of the room.

"Miss Swinton?"

She stirred and nodded. "How good of you to call on me. It has been long since I have received anyone. That is, save James."

The door onto the passage opened and in stepped Dr. Nuttall.

Chapter Twenty

I was stunned into temporary silence. "Why are you here?" I finally stammered.

"I was about to ask you the very same question," he riposted.

"Perhaps we should step into the passageway," I said with an anxious look for Miss Swinton.

"There is nothing you can say I have not heard before," she directed. "I am reduced to renting rooms in the house of another. Dr. Nuttall is good enough to provide the necessary funds. This makes me unspeakably exceptionable. So, as you can see, the worst has already happened."

My hands curled into fists. "How can you have allowed this?" I demanded.

"You do not understand! It could not be helped!" he insisted, his face red with anger or shame, I could not say.

I turned and stormed from the room. Was this the fate that awaited Jane? Was I no better than the physician? At least I had not succumbed to the same depravity as my cousin, Eve.

"Wait!" Dr. Nuttall called as he came after me. "There is a child. My *only* child."

I was again without words. "Then why have you not married her?" My words exploded from me as I turned from him in disgust and started down the stairs. "What business do you have hanging about the Andersens?" I threw over my shoulder. "Miss Swinton ought to be living in your house in the country with you, not reduced to living out her days over the mews in a room that smells of rot!"

He clattered down the stairs after me. "I thought—hoped and prayed—my wife might still be alive. How could I marry another? But now, matters are different. It is why I am here today."

"And what of Mrs. Andersen?" I demanded as I strode briskly to the front door. "Was that not the story you told? The reason you could not marry her?" I was angry, my voice raised. "Might you have got her with child, as well? Then you would have two families to house, both out of sight of the world and the people of your village. Have you killed her for that? Or was it to get her out of the way so you might have her daughter as well?"

He stared at me as if I had run mad, but he stopped following me. I gave him one last scathing look and took myself from the house. I was angrier than I could remember ever having been, even when Eve had threatened me about Jane. Worse, I knew it was because of her—because I would be reducing her to this, if Eve did not step up and offer for her. And what if she refused him? Worse, what if she did not? Every one of my thoughts led to a brick wall that held me at bay.

I finally climbed aboard the carriage and took my aching head between my hands, my hair caught between my fingers. The physician was despicable. Eve was despicable. What was I? I rocked back and forth as my thoughts and emotions swung from one extreme to another. I should run away with Jane and live out our days in the country. I should warn Jane of what was coming, what sort of man Eve was; the distasteful consequences of the article in the newspaper. I should allow to come what may and forget her entirely.

Gradually, my roiling thoughts calmed, and I was able to put my feelings aside to determine what should be done about Dr. Nuttall. Was he guilty of murder? He could have over-dosed Mrs. Andersen in such a way her daughter felt responsible. If so, had he also killed Lady Marlowe, or was that truly an accident? I knew something was missing, that a piece of the puzzle was yet required in order to see things clearly. In my mind, I still had three suspects: Dr. Nuttall, whom I thought of as the Fiendish Physician; Miss Andersen, the Sorrowful Orphan; and Sir Thomas, the Protective Father. Which one was a killer?

Upon my arrival home, I went straight to the salon to pour myself a drink. I knew that I was indulging too much, but I could not bring myself to care. I found it necessary to quiet my emotions, so I might think about murder rather than the breaking of my heart. Most of the bottles were empty, but there was a new, unopened one of Burgundy. I thought perhaps Hatch did not hate me as much as I had believed. In retrospect, I ought to have questioned the notion more thoroughly; I most often had to ring for a new bottle of libations of every kind.

'Twas fortunate for me Hatch entered what he thought was an empty room to put it in order. I was nearly gone but had enough presence of mind to take steps to save my life. "Send for Dr. Nuttall," I managed to grind out before I emptied my stomach upon the Persian carpet that had adorned the room since my great-grandfather's time.

I knew no more until I found it urgent to once again cast up my accounts onto my forebears' lovely rug. However, to my surprise, a commode appeared as if from nowhere. I made prompt use of it, lay my head back, and closed my eyes. "Jack," I murmured, thinking how very predictable, steady, and faithful he was. I opened my eyes to verify he was present. He was, as was Dr. Nuttall, and Hatch who hovered in the background.

"He shall live," the physician said to the butler.

He nodded and quit the room. I thought he looked sorrier than not.

"What has happened?" I asked.

"You were poisoned. This lad rode like the fastest jockey to find me. We arrived just in time to give you the proper remedies. I believe you have heaved up most of the poison—enough that you shall live."

I put my hand on Jack's. "Good boy. Now, retrieve the bottle—'twas the Burgundy—and discover how it got into this house."

He gave me a short nod, collected the bottle, and burst from the room.

I turned my attention to the doctor. "You have saved my life. I might be wrong, but I believe it means you were not the one who wished to kill me."

"Of course, I did not wish to kill you! If I had, I might have done it that day I struck you on the head."

I chuckled weakly. "But that was before I railed at you earlier today. Or was that yesterday?" I turned my head to look at him.

"It is late, but not that late." He put his hand to my forehead and then checked my pulse at the wrist. "It had been rather sluggish, but it is picking up. Here." He helped me to sit up and put a glass of water to my lips.

I pressed them together and batted the glass away. "I am not that certain!" I shook my head to clear the grogginess, then gave him a good, long stare. "Say something that shall convince me you are not the one who killed Mrs. Andersen, Lady Marlowe, or, for that matter, your lovely wife."

He stared at me in astonishment. "I hadn't the slightest idea I was under suspicion."

I refused to reply, only glared at him unrelentingly.

"Ah, well, let me see. Firstly, I was out of the country when my wife died. It is with unspeakable sorrow that I think back on the times I have sat in that house, slept in my bed, ate meals between the same walls that held my wife's body captive." He shuddered. "I have no wish to speak of it. As for Mrs. Andersen, I had an affection for her, as well as

242

her daughter. I was drawn to them and their tragic story. There was something about them that compelled one to help them."

I grunted. "There is truth in that."

"I had no wish to marry either of them, however. In fact, Miss Swinton and I are to be wed as soon as may be."

I nodded rather drunkenly. "May I be the first to congratulate you?"

"Thank you. As for Mrs. Andersen, I do believe her daughter could very well have accidentally overdosed her mother. It is not uncommon. It happens more often than you know."

"And you cover it up when it does?"

He drew a deep breath and nodded slightly. "It is best. Accusing an innocent party who is grieving the death of a loved one will not change anything; it will only deepen the sorrow."

I reluctantly agreed with him. "And what of Lady Marlowe? Was her death an accident?"

His face darkened. "There, I am guilty."

I looked at him, startled. "You killed her?"

He shook his head. "I lied about not having been there. I overheard them conversing. Lady Marlowe was concerned about Miss Andersen's expectations now that she had become Sir Thomas' heir."

"She is his true daughter. Did you know that?"

"I have deduced it. Miss Andersen was livid. She resented that Lady Marlowe accused her of manipulating Sir

Thomas, making him change his will. Why it would matter either way, I cannot guess. She is meant to inherit what is left only after both he and his wife had died. Lady Marlowe said as much. It seemed to be the final stroke."

"Miss Andersen pushed her?"

"I was in my room and did not see it for myself. I heard them leave a chamber across the passage and they went to the stairs. Lady Marlowe was late for a dinner party. I could hear the rustling of her silks as she strode down the passage. Hannah was right behind her, shouting at her. And then I heard a series of thuds and a scream."

I pondered. "Is there no way to know precisely what happened?"

"Not unless she confesses. There is no way to prove she did or did not. But it is my opinion she is a killer."

"I feel much the same despite having less reason to know it. What can be done?"

"We must learn what we can about the bottle—who delivered it, where it was purchased, an investigation of the insides, if possible. Depending on what we find, we must contact the authorities."

I nodded. "Very well. I thank you for your candor. And for saving my life."

"I shall take myself off now," he said with a bow, "but I shall return to review your progress tomorrow. I shall be interested in knowing what is learned about the bottle as well."

I watched him walk away and forgot him almost before the door closed. He was no longer a concern of mine.

I did not see Jack again that night. I supposed he was carrying out my instructions, but his absence vexed me. A footman appeared to see me upstairs to bed. I awoke the next morning to find Jack standing by my side, watching me intently.

"Gad sakes, boy!" I cried in alarm, despite being desperately relieved to see him. It had occurred to me I had sent him to his death in my quest for the truth.

"The bottle was purchased by a Miss Andersen," he said, as if reciting a piece of poetry.

My heart sank, but I was not surprised. "Well done," I praised him. "Later we shall discuss what is to be done about it."

"Like wot?"

"Such as contact the authorities. But first we must have further proof." I held my hand out to him for assistance.

He helped me to rise and dress. The altered pantaloons had been fetched home whilst I was out, and I refused to quit my chamber until the ring was placed in its secret pocket. Then Jack held on to my elbow as he walked me down the stairs to my favored divan in the salon. It was degrading, but I found I did not care. I made myself comfortable and looked around the room. Everything was brighter and lighter and infinitely lovelier after my brush with death. I noticed the Persian had been replaced with something wholly inferior. I was grateful not to have to endure the odor of my having cast up my accounts.

I had slept late and was forced to take my breakfast from a rolling cart when Mrs. S. entered.

"My darling boy! How good that you are alive!"

I dropped my fork onto the plate with a clatter. "How did you know?"

"It doesn't matter," she soothed. "Lady Jersey shall never forgive me if I were to give her away."

I grabbed my cup and gulped my coffee. "I suppose everyone, including the killer, will now know I yet live," I complained.

"Oh! I had not thought of that!" she cried. Rushing to my side, she wedged herself between me and the cart with an alarming rattle of dishes, took my hand, and held it to her cheek. "But you are alive! That is what matters!"

'Twas then that the door opened, and my would-be murderer entered.

I bolted to my feet, my knee colliding with the cart which rolled away with a clatter. "Miss Andersen, what brings you here?" I was very much afraid, but I knew I had to remain calm. Silently, I prayed she was done with the work of death.

Miss Andersen's face bleached white. "Was it ill-bred of me to come?" she asked faintly.

"Not at all," I lied. A reproach seemed a small matter over which to kill a man, but she had killed for less.

"But of course, you should not have, young lady!" Mrs.

S. chided. "This sort of behavior puts you quite beyond the pale."

I shoved her rather ruthlessly aside so that I acted as her shield. (An inadequate one, all things considered.)

Miss Andersen merely looked struck. "I ought to have realized that on my own." She choked on the bitter laughter that rose from her throat.

"You are hysterical," I pointed out. The rays of the late afternoon sun warmed our backs and, I hoped, prevented Miss Andersen from seeing us clearly, should she have a muff gun on her person.

She laughed again, a high-pitched affair that did nothing to alter my premonition of doom. "I suppose I ought to have sent a messenger to request that you wait on me at Marlowe House," she said, her tone astringent. "Now I shall be castigated. 'Tis a pity! There is little I care for more than Society's good opinion."

I marveled that she believed she yet had the opportunity to win Society's approval but refrained from saying so. "Why is that, Miss Andersen?"

She gave me an over-bright smile and tilted her head, as does a bird in a cage. "It is important to me that I am thought of as a lady."

"Well-behaved young ladies do not kill their mothers," I pointed out at my peril.

Her face hardened. "I have told you, it was an accident. How you could think otherwise, I cannot understand. She was everything to me. Everything!" She jumped to her feet and began to pace the room. Between her fingers she clutched the strings of a reticule weighed down by an unknown burden.

Transfixed, I watched as it bounced against her skirts with every step. I attempted to calculate the possibility of its being a gun. Ready to leap to the side at any moment, I plunged onward with my words. "Please accept my apologies, Miss Andersen. I believed you when you claimed to have no desire to end her life, and I believe you now."

Her countenance fell as she collapsed into a chair and burst into tears. "How I yearn for her! I cannot imagine a future without her!"

As I was certain Miss Andersen had no future, I offered no words of comfort. "How long do you suppose you shall go free before you are exposed for the murderer you are?" It was the death of Lady Marlowe to which I referred.

The tears stopped as abruptly as they had begun. "I have never been exposed for a murderer; not once!" she insisted.

"What is this? You regret no one has learned of your perfidy? Is it fame you seek?"

She scowled. "No! It's only that I have been a killer for the longest time and no one has even begun to guess."

"Whatever can you mean?" Despite my reservations, I was beyond curious. So was Mrs. S. Her breath came fast and hard, and she leaned so far forward at Miss Andersen's words that she nearly unbalanced me.

"The first time I killed," she said, her voice thin and higher than I had heard it, "I was quite young." She looked straight through me, past the scar that marked me, through the window at my back and on into the light of day. I was young, jus' a lit'le girl, really," she said, her proper pronunciation deteriorating.

Considering her known methods of murder, I dismissed both as options unavailable to a child. "How can that be? It was, I am certain, far too difficult an endeavor."

She smiled, as if enjoying a fond memory. "Oh, I was clever, e'en then. I didn' wan' to do it, not really." She focused her attention again on my face. "And yet, I ha' ne'er regretted it. It was necess'ry; very necess'ry."

Beyond her expensively bonneted head, the door to the room slowly opened a crack. Jack's eye was visible in the void. I nodded very slightly, and he soundlessly shut it. I knew he would do as I expected, though I doubted when the local constable arrived he would be astute enough to incarcerate Miss Andersen for her crimes. Of more immediate concern was my rescue; who could know what plans she had for the heavy bulge in her reticule?

"And why was that?" I said in conversational tones that were utterly feigned.

"I wished to ha' Mama to mysel' o'course. Didn' you know?" She gave me a queer look, as if she suddenly doubted my intelligence. "Bu', more than that, I was ashamed o'him. Of his cowardice. Of his willingness to flee in the face of danger." Her speech grew more precise. "I would never do anything so cowardly. Am I not here now?" Bravado shone on her face.

249

"I fear I do not quite understand. You had said you knew your father was innocent of suicide the last time we spoke of such matters." I ran a mental finger along the inside of my collar. I could feel the dampness of the linen against my neck; the scent of sweat mingled with starch and shaving cream rose into the air. It was most unpleasant. Outside the birds trilled their spring courting exactly as if I were not pinned in the glare of a killer.

"No. No!" she cried. "You know nothing!" She laughed as she again rose to her feet and paced about. "I had not thought I would ever speak of it to anyone. It is too shameful, but I find I cannot depart without someone knowing the truth."

My patience was thinning, and my head felt as if it were clamped in a vise. "Of what matter do we speak?" Where she planned to go upon her departure was of decreasing interest to me.

She turned to look me squarely in the eye. "About the first time I killed. Haven't you guessed?" When I continued to stare at her, perplexed, she uttered a harsh laugh. "Oh, that is rich! I have given you all the clues required. Or are you less clever than I had supposed?"

"I cannot claim to know how clever you think me," I said shortly. "Perhaps you ought to assume I am not clever in the least. The death of your mother, then, was not the first for which you were responsible?"

"No, it was not." She stared at me, goggle-eyed. "Oh come, come, my lord! It is not so very difficult!"

A notion that had begun to take shape in my mind now came into sharper focus. "No, I do not believe it," I said mildly. I suppose I hoped she made such imprecise claims only for attention.

"Believe it, my lord! It is the truth!" The expression in her eyes was clear; without guile.

Belief came upon me in one fell swoop and my mouth fell open in shock. "But how?" I gasped.

"It was not so difficult," she said with a coquettish toss of her head. "I had thought to save him, but when I heard how she cried out for the coward I knew what I had to do. I sat on the ground between her and him so that my actions would not be seen and studied the way he hung from just three fingers. They were red and white and slippery with effort." She shivered. "I merely peeled them back, one by one. I have often wondered why he didn't cry out; never revealed what it was I was about. I suppose he had no wish to deprive Mama of her love for me. And then, so very quickly, it was too late. He was gone."

If Mrs. S. had not been standing behind me, I would surely have collapsed to the floor. As it was I felt as if I were falling, deeper and deeper into her natural-born cushions. Oh-so-slowly, falling forever. "You killed your father."

She heaved a sigh of satisfaction and smiled; an eerie, macabre curving of the lips. "Yes." She tightened her grip on the object in the lace-trimmed reticule. "And now there is nothing left to do but ensure that the story comes to an end."

251

As she opened the drawstring bag I took Mrs. S. by the arm, pushed her down to lie behind the settee opposite, and threw myself on top. I braced myself for the sound of shots fired and, when they did not come, risked a peek above a row of tufted trim.

I was wrong; it was not a gun, but a knife that Miss Andersen held in her hand. I froze, unable to stir. Her gaze met mine for what seemed forever, though it must have been less than seconds. Forcing away my horror of the wicked blade, I struggled to get to my feet without treading on the terrified Mrs. S. I kept my vision trained on the deadly steel as Miss Andersen put the tip to her chest just above her properly donned fichu.

"'Tis what Quality would do, is that not so?" She pushed the knife ever so slightly, so that it nearly pierced the alabaster skin of her bosom. "There is no ascending the steps of the gallows for the *ton*."

Finally free of entanglement with Mrs. S. I rushed to rescue Miss Andersen, but I arrived too late; she fell in a heap at my feet. I wanted to gather her in my arms as I had another killer I had known who had chosen a similar way out, but something held me back. Perhaps it was that she would have feared it was not entirely proper. Instead, I knelt at her side and examined her for any signs of life. When I determined that there were none, I gently closed the lids over her sightless eyes.

In the end it was not the authorities who came to my aid, but Evelyn. I assumed he hoped to avoid further staining of my honor by the demise of Miss Andersen in my salon. When he arrived, he took one look at the scene and ordered me to depart. I might still be standing there, aghast at what had happened, if Jack hadn't dragged me out the door, a bulging valise under his arm. I allowed him to lead until we obtained the walkway outside the house. That was when I turned to take in what I thought might very well be the end of my life in London. After all, Evelyn had never done me any favors before; I dared not trust him now.

Chapter Twenty-One

I passed a restless night in a hotel whilst Jack roamed the halls as a lookout for any danger. In the morning, I collected from my tailor what had been made up of my wedding clothes and sent Jack to procure me a trunk. We boarded ship for Africa, where it no longer mattered whether Miss Andersen's father had killed himself. They were all gone now; his so-called daughter had seen to that.

When I thought it safe to return to the Continent, I perused the periodicals only to read of my cousin's marriage to Jane. It was said they honeymooned in Paris, the very city in which I found myself. I left immediately for Italy. As I signed the ledger at the desk of my favorite Venice hotel, my attention was caught by a stir at the entrance. It was them. I shall never forget the look of hurt—nay, sorrow—in Jane's eyes when my glance brushed past hers.

It was the first time I had reason to suspect my rejection of her hurt very much indeed. The pain nearly doubled me, but I was relieved, too, that Miss Andersen's death had in no way harmed my dearest Jane. It was then I realized that Eve had no care for my reputation at all whatsoever. It was for Jane that he tidied the disarray caused by Miss Andersen's dying.

It was autumn before I received notice from Eve that there was no danger to me if I returned to England. I chose to do so. That's how little I cared if his claim could be trusted. By the time I arrived, the joys of the Little Season were over. There was naught to do but settle into the sort of life one endures in a depopulated London; the journey to Alders was one too far for me at the time. I passed the days drinking and devising new means to avoid Mrs. S. I did not dare face her after throwing her behind the settee on that ill-fated day. However, she had no such qualms.

"My Lord Trevelin!" she barked one afternoon upon cornering me where I sat over a pedestrian meal of tea and scones. She was overjoyed to find me in residence. "It has been far too long!"

"On the contrary, Mrs. S," I said, rising with an urbane smile.

"What was that?" she asked, her hand cupped around her ear as she took up her customary seat next to me.

Unsure as to whether her further loss of hearing would add to my comfort or lessen it, I sighed. "How was the Little Season for you?" I asked as I folded the periodical I had been reading. "Delightful, I hope!"

"You shall be too glad you have missed it," she said with a smile too smug for my liking. "It was quite illuminoting!"

I suppressed another sigh. "Perhaps you had best enlighten me."

"Well!" She smiled coyly, as if she were being courted rather than tolerated. "It is rather why I have come!"

"You have never before required a reason," I said with a mildness I did not feel.

She batted my hand in what I suspect she felt to be affection. "It is said there is a young miss who lives in a little house in the country."

I suspected my ensuing frown was most fearsome. "Am I meant to know the identity of this young miss?"

She shrugged her abundance of shoulder. "It is difficult to imagine you do not know her name when it is said you pay the rent each quarter."

I felt my face burn with righteous indignation mingled with unwarranted shame. "This is being bruited about town?" I asked through gritted teeth.

"Indeed, but I have said it must not be true. You could not have been the reason for her ruin!"

The inn was of the most deplorable. One look at the disheveled owner and her filthy children and all was revealed. That any were forced to take refuge in such a place filled me with horror. The innkeeper led me down a dank hallway and rapped upon a door.

A timid voice bade us enter and I peered through the doorway into the darkened room. "Thank you, that is all." I placed a coin in her hand and turned to the girl huddled on the bed. Its torn and dirty drapery was only slightly worse than the clothing she wore. "Do you remember me?" I asked.

"Yes," she said in a voice full of resignation.

I stepped into the room and seated myself in a chair. The cold of it seeped through my greatcoat and I restrained a shiver. "I have heard it said your father would have nothing more to do with you after...what happened." I hated speaking such loathsome words. "I have been looking for you ever since."

She gazed at me in surprise. "I had thought you different from other men."

Words of indignation sprang to my lips, but I bit them back. "Not in the way you suppose. It is true, however, that I mean you no harm."

She frowned. "I had also thought you too clever to make such a trite remark."

"Trite it may be, but that does not render it false." I looked about and saw that she had very little. "Gather your things. When you have finished, I shall meet you below stairs."

Her expression was one of suspicion. "Are we to go elsewhere, then?"

"Yes, you are," I said, and swept from the room.

She found me in the taproom far sooner than I had expected in my cynicism. I led her out into the yard, where a coach and four waited. Tossing her pitiful bag to the coachman to stow, I gave her my instructions. "You are to be taken to a house in Yorkshire. You will be comfortable there, and safe. The dun for rent shall come to me, and you will have a quarterly allowance for food and clothing. There shall be space for a vegetable patch and a chicken or two, should you desire it."

Her face, as I spoke, grew soft and tears started in her eyes. "It is far more than I expected. You are very kind." She turned to the open door of the coach but paused before she had put a foot to the steps. "When shall I expect to see you again?"

I thought she could not surprise me more than she had already. "Never," I said.

"Your friends?" she asked, puzzled.

"No. I shall tell no one of your direction," I replied, equally puzzled. "I urge you to inform your father, however. I cannot speak to his capacity for forgiveness, but I am persuaded your mother shall be most happy to know you are in want of nothing."

She seemed to sag against the coach door as the true meaning of my words sank in. It was only then I realized she had expected to be a kept woman. She cried in earnest now. "My lord, you are different from other men. I thought I should never again look on any man with favor after what Mr. Rogers-Reimann did to me, the life he cursed me to, but you have given me hope."

My heart swelled with gratitude. To undo the evil my cousin had done had been my aim all along. "'Tis nothing," I said gruffly. "Only...be happy."

I turned away before she had fully climbed aboard. I heard the creak and sway of the carriage as the coachman climbed onto the box. With a crack of his whip, the horses leaped into action. The wheels crushed the gravel of the yard as the whole of it rumbled out of my life. The deed was done, the wrong reversed, and all would be well.

"What is her name?" I asked dully, despite a wild hope such information had never been divulged.

"I believe it was a Miss Ashley, Miss Sarah Ashley, but

it's a rather common-sounding name. I could not say that was it, for certain."

I could. My heart fell into my stomach. I had willingly taken on the shame of jilting Jane to spare her the dishonor threatened by the man who became her husband. But how was I to brave this new storm? "And who has given tongue to such a tale?" I asked lightly. Nothing had taxed my talents as a thespian more.

"Who else but that cad, Rogers-Reimann?"

I might have spared her the question.

"You are not to worry, my lord! It is a well-known fact that gentlemen have their weaknesses. I suppose there is not a lord in parliament who does not keep a mistress!"

"You are correct about that, Mrs. S.," I said grimly. "Almost."

"No?" she asked, somewhat aghast. "Well, as for the other matter—no one shall believe it was you who disgraced Miss Ashley. I shall tell everyone I know that Rogers-Reimann is a liar!"

"And risk that he shall find some way to ruin you, as well? You shall be cast from the homes of your friends and neighbors."

"I shall not be cast from your home, my lord, of that I am certain."

"No!" I insisted, in terror I should be Mrs. Smurthwaite's last and only friend. "You must not. Indeed," I said, taking her plump hands in mine, "I cannot allow it. It is too much of a sacrifice."

Her face suffused with color as she leaned towards me and kissed my cheek, the one above the scar. It had been long since any had touched me there; touched me anywhere, save Jack when he shaved my chin. To my chagrin, tears started in my eyes.

She took her hands from mine and rose to her feet. "I must go. I am expecting my hairdresser to tame my tresses."

Doubtfully, I eyed the puffs of downy white that already inadequately concealed her head. "Yes, of course. And thank you, Mrs. Smurthwaite. I look forward to seeing you again—when your locks are tamer." I gave her a bow and she ambled from the room of her own volition for the first time since I had known her.

Numb, I collected the ring from its pocket in the waistband of my pantaloons and put it upon my finger. I repeated the familiar litany: Never again would I allow myself to forget how I am perceived by others. I am a jilt, a knave, the ruination of maidens. No one shall ever trust me with their daughter ever again. I shall remain alone and childless.

Hope had been the price I paid in granting it to Miss Ashley. I should never again feel it swell my heart. The very taste of it turned to ashes on my tongue.

In want of immediate privacy, I took the stairs two at a time, gripping my ringed finger as I went. I hoped the pain of it cutting into my flesh would obscure the growing agony in my heart, but it was not enough. I fell against the door to my chamber, forced it open, dropped to my knees, and gave vent to my feelings in a bout of weeping.

"Trev, I am here." Willy stood by my side, his hand outstretched.

I fancied I could feel the heat of it as it hovered just above my head. "Why? Why did he do it? I did what he asked, as much as it pained me—and, oh God," I growled, "did it pain me! But he couldn't be satisfied until he had taken away everything, every measure of what I had gained after his last assault on my good name!"

Willy's voice seemed so full of tears that I expected the hot droplets to fall and mingle with my own. "Some men are a body of evil where no light can enter. But, you have not lost everything. I am here, Trev, and I shall always be your friend."

He was right. A truer friend I had never known, unless it was Jack. I knew he stood, hesitating, just outside the door I had failed to shut tight behind me in my misery. Struggling to hold back my sobs long enough to instruct him, I told him to fetch hot water for a bath. I knew he would do as I asked, and be a long time about it, too. I was not yet ready to tell him about Willy. He would think me a lunatic; I thought that perhaps I was, and not for the first time.

"Trev." Willy was again in his chair by the window, his face etched with sorrow. "This shall pass."

I looked away, unable to bear his pain alongside my own. "Whether it does or does not, it is of no consequence."

"But it is, old fellow! In the meantime, what does it

matter what people say? You know the truth. I know the truth. Even that boot boy of yours doubtless knows the truth."

"The truth! And what is the truth?" I demanded angrily. "That should Jane hear of it, she should learn to despise me as well?"

"'Twas doubtless one of his aims. She shall make him a far more comfortable wife if she does not believe herself in love with you."

I felt the defeat flood me, body and spirit. "Perhaps it is best. She shall be happier if she thinks me a cad and unworthy of her."

"I do think so. As for the rest, it shall be a nine-days wonder. You are a marquis! Of what consequence would it be if you did have a mistress set up in a cottage somewhere? Most believe it is true of all men with money and power or, barring those, enough charm."

And yet my title had spared me very little in the past. It puzzled me. I rose wearily to my feet and sat on the bed, eying the ring upon my finger. "I have always hoped to marry for love. The world is full of unions blessed by riches and position; I had wanted more for myself."

"And why is that so far beyond your reach?" he scoffed.

"Perhaps it is not too much to expect someone to love me. But shall she love me? The true me? I cannot bear to share my life with someone who sees only the scars," I whispered.

"Perhaps you fear the one who cannot love is you." His voice was gentle and without reproach.

I pondered his words and knew them to be true. How could I love anyone as I had loved Jane? The sobs started in my lungs, wracking my ribs, building and building until I could not hope to hold them back. Slowly, I fell, like a tree in the forest until my face came to rest against the counterpane. It was on that fallow field I lost the battle. All the unshed tears I had held back for far too long came forth in a flood.

I wept for Mrs. Nuttall and her unborn babe; for Dr. Nuttall who had lost the wife for whom he still longed. I wept for Willy and his brother John, neither of whom had deserved to die. Most of all, I wept for Julian, the boy who had lost his parents too soon and had never properly mourned them. Finally, I wept for myself, the man who had lost everything, including the only woman to whom he had truly given his heart.

As the sobs continued to pound my ribs, I slid from the bed onto the floor. It was where Jack found me some hours later, cried out, spent, and utterly alone. He woke me with his finger beneath my nose in his quest to learn if I yet breathed. It smelled of a rancid mingling of starch and onions. Coughing, I swatted at it.

He jumped away from me as if from a live coal. "Beggin' yer pardon," he murmured.

I rolled over onto my side and looked towards him, attempting to make him out in the glare of the candle he held. It was the only light in the room. "Help me up. I must see Jane."

He dropped his head. "Why 'er?"

"What business is that of yours? Just do as I say," I urged as I stumbled to my feet. I watched him as he went to the sconce on the wall and lit the candle closest to the clothespress. I thought he would open the doors and draw out a clean shirt, but instead he turned to face me, his face set and determined.

"There's summat I ought to 'ave tol' you. A lon' time ago."

My stomach tightened with dread. Berating myself for a fool, I reminded myself that the worst had already happened. "Go on," I said, my voice hoarse.

He drew a deep breath. "A day or p'raps two, after I took yer note to Leavitt House...it was so long ago, I don' rightly 'member..." His expression was anxious.

"Yes?"

"It was your lady, Jane. Leastways, I think it was 'er. She and a man—she called him Walter."

"Yes! Where did you see them?" Despite my silent admonitions, the tightening of my stomach worsened.

"They came to see ya, here. I was nearby, but I hid mysel' and watched. Hatch said you wern' at home, and I do believe 'twas true; you were ou'. But whilst he went to see, they spoke to each other." He gave me another look of trepidation.

"What did they say?"

"He said that it wer no use, that ev'n if he hadn' dropped her, their papa wou' not allow her to marry him, and she said tha' she would do anythin', even run away wi' him, that she loved him. That's what she said—him. Did she mean you?"

I nodded, my legs weak, my head spinning.

Jack swallowed and looked away. "Then Hatch came back and said you were ou'. They both gave 'im their cards and he slipped 'em into his pocket. I never saw 'em again—he never 'ad me take 'em to you. I'm guessin' he never 'ad a footman take 'em to you, neither."

"Jane." I dropped my face into my hands. "She loves me still." At least until she got wind of her husband's latest attack on my reputation. As Society perceived me, I was no longer a man of whom she could be proud. No more Eve, and yet it was his children she would bring into the world. I stumbled to Willy's chair and frenziedly ran my hand across the seat. "Willy, where are you?" I cared not that Jack was witness to my formerly furtive madness. "Willy! How has this happened? Tell me! How?" I curled my fists and shook them at the window beyond which lay the houses where dwelt the finest of Society. "I am Julian Silvester, Marquis of Trevelin!" I roared. "Why are you against me?"

'Twas but a matter of months before I learned the answer to my questions. Oh, how I wished I had not.

The End

When the snow-trapped guests at a Christmas house party put a murder suspect under lock and key, Trev has no choice but to prove the innocence of their captive—one Julian Silvester, Marquis of Trevelin. Coming soon: THE MURDER IN MIRTH, book three in The Lord Trevelin Mysteries.

About the Author

Award-winning, best-selling author Heidi Ashworth lives with her family in the San Francisco Bay Area. She writes sweet, traditional Regency romance, romantic comedy, and historical mystery. The Scandal in Honor is the second book in The Lord Trevelin Mysteries. Look for The Murder in Mirth soon!

Review The Scandal in Honor: http://a.co/iwNqXWc

Sign up for my newsletter at The Scribbling Divas: https://tinyurl.com/jknfanp

Amazon Page: https://www.amazon.com/default/e/B001JSDUX6

Facebook: https://www.facebook.com/authorheidiashworth/

Twitter:@AshworthHeidi

Bookbub: https://www.bookbub.com/profile/heidi-ashworth

Website/Blog: www.HeidiAshworth.blogspot.com

Pinterest: https://www.pinterest.com/ashworth0763/

Goodreads: https://www.goodreads.com/author/show/2052146.Heidi_Ashworth